BLUE MOON
RISING

RENA' AVERETT

PUBLISHED BY BOOKBABY
2023

Blue Moon Rising

Copyright © 2023 Rena' Averett

The Holy Bible, New International Version ®, NIV ® Copyright © 2011 by Biblica, Inc. ® Used by permission. All rights reserved.

ISBN (Print Edition): 979-8-35091-622-5
ISBN (eBook Edition): 979-8-35091-623-2

Lord, You are my God;
I will exalt you, and praise your name,
for in perfect faithfulness you have done wonderful things,
things planned long ago.
Isaiah 25:1

To Sherry:
Your friendship made the difference.
Thank you.

To the Reader

A stained-glass window is designed with panels of varied shapes, sizes and colors. Viewed individually, each shard lacks significance, meaning, purpose. Yet, in the hands of the artist, he assigns value. Then he creates.

He works until the vision is achieved, determining the perfect placement of each piece. Each sliver holds meaning and adds to the overall beauty. The collaboration of many parts into the whole.

So it is with *Blue Moon Rising*. Though fiction, the story is inspired by my own journey. The artist, my Heavenly Father, used seemingly unrelated events, encounters and disappointments to create something beautiful. He assigned value even where there seemed to be no value, and worked all the pieces together for good.

Enjoy the story. If you find yourself in the pages of *Blue Moon Rising*, be assured, our faithful Heavenly Father is there with you. Be encouraged. Be challenged. Be inspired.

BLUE MOON
RISING

Chapter One

---≈---

R achel sat up straight away, dropping her feet to the wool rug at her bedside. She rubbed her toes deep into the soft pile. Her body crouched,
head bowed, heart racing.

This sleep had been hard. Deep. The sleep that comes from tired emotions
rather than a worn body. Naps were few and far between at The Renaissance
House. At least for her.

The warmth of the afternoon sun on the old Southern farmhouse
reminded of spring's arrival. Rachel retrieved a handkerchief from under
her pillow. She wiped the wet strands away from her face and dabbed the
dampness from the nape of her neck.

Rachel's heartbeat slowed as she gathered her bearings. She refolded the
cloth to display the bold monogrammed letters. *JS*. Her eyes rested on the
black threads for a few moments before she tucked the cloth back in place
under her pillow.

She stood with caution. Though in pretty good shape for a nearly fifty-
year-old, bursitis in her left hip would reach out rather unexpectedly. She

drew up the blind, leaning her full weight on the window casing. She gazed to the rolling acres of Avery Farms that extended behind the home.

It seemed just yesterday she had looked out over the same barren field. Desiring change. Growth. And choosing it. A year had so quickly come and gone. She was thankful for spring. Winter months were Rachel's least favorite. The dry earth revealing only remnants of the past season's bounty. Stalks…stems…dirt. A season of dormancy that could bring uneasy, low emotions and a longing for something new—anything new. Rachel's winter had been longer than it should.

Come, spring! Please, come! It had answered.

The ground had been prepared. It was ready to receive the seeds that would bring the expected harvest. The field would again be green and lush. She breathed a deep, satisfying breath. *Tomorrow.*

Rachel's phone alerted of the afternoon schedule. A few hurried moments were spent regaining a physical presentation appropriate for her role as host. She twisted her wavey, blonde locks up and off her neck with a ruby-studded clip. A hairpiece too charming for a regular day of work. With one last glance, she closed the door to her private living area and rushed to the kitchen to tend the chores.

The door of the oven was pulled down a third time. Cookies would be served at three o'clock. Though the timer was still ticking, the quirky oven was rarely compliant. Ten minutes was not enough time for baking. One minute more seemed too much. Rachel reached in and took hold of the baking sheet with the end of her worn apron and placed the confections on the stovetop.

Rachel's Renaissance cookies had become a favorite for her guests. She wanted them to be unforgettable each time. Oatmeal, chocolate chips, and pecans. Pecans she gathered from her own trees. As the baking progressed, the aroma wafted through the house drawing the guests to the gathering room in anticipation.

Today, there was only one guest.

The German cuckoo clock hanging over the Depression-era buffet announced the time. The Fraulein exited the double doors of the timepiece and proceeded to twirl as the track moved her about. By the time the wooden figure's performance was complete and the triple cuckoo had ended, Rachel had the refreshments arranged on the buffet.

A homegrown bouquet of early gardenias accented the display. Rachel's favorite. Her heart would never release the memory of the first delicate, white blooms he presented on her doorstep. His blue eyes focused, body pressed in. His soft lips delivering an ever-so-gentle kiss to her cheekbone. His warm breath on her ear. A shiver coursed through her body even now.

Rachel took a deep, cleansing breath and returned to the task before her. It was teatime. Though tea was rarely the drink of choice for her guests, the term seemed to suit her bed-and-breakfast patrons.

The lone female guest was already in the gathering room when her host entered. The musical pronouncement of the time did not seem to rouse her from her intrigue, nor did the presence of a second person. Her movement was methodical. She tended to every detail of the layers of vintage décor on the craftsman-style fireplace shelving. She touched the artifacts, picked them up, investigated them, and then carefully returned them to their assigned places.

The gathering room had a defining stature, with ceilings reaching ten feet. The ceilings and walls were of unpainted pine, original to the century-old home. Rachel's own hands had uncovered this stunning treasure when she removed the brittle paper and cheesecloth from its 1920s walls and discolored tiles from the ceiling. It had been a labor of love that had revealed the natural beauty others strove to recreate.

Paintings were double-hung in the English cottage style. Turn-of-the-century furniture was coupled with mid-century modern pieces that were purposeful yet intended for comfort.

Windows larger than six feet flanked the home. Filtered light was abundant and changed throughout the day with the shifting of the sun. The sunsets of the west-facing gathering room were a bonus neither Rachel nor her guests could resist. Cozy seating invited observers to linger.

A maple dining table handed down by Rachel's mother stood adorned with a blue and white checkered tablecloth. Each occasion of passing found Rachel tracking her fingers over the delicate cloth, her mind stepping back to a distant time and place. Delicious homemade breakfasts of The Renaissance House were presented here. Service was daily at eight o'clock sharp.

The gabled front porch extended from the dining area, with satisfying views of livestock and barns in the distance. Early risers, with coffee in hand, often reported the soothing sounds of cattle lowing in the adjoining field, hidden by the low morning fog. Farm life.

"Oh my! Hello!" The young lady approached and extended her hand. "I apologize for my rudeness. My mother says I get lost in the details. I must admit, your home has enough details to keep me distracted for a long time." Rachel smiled and attempted a response. Her guest interrupted. "It's hard to put into words, but the atmosphere makes me want to nuzzle deep in that leather armchair and relax, which, I assure you, I never do! There's a peaceful charm here. It draws me in."

The guest looked Rachel square in the face. "Wow! If you could bottle this!"

Rachel chuckled at the candid expressions of this energetic young woman, who reminded her of her own daughters. Her chatter was delightful and welcomed.

"Well, Samantha, you take a seat in the armchair, and I'll get your cookies. Milk?" The young lady nodded and willingly obeyed.

"It reminds me of my grandma's place. Without the smell of old people, of course." A sheepish look came over the young woman's face. "No disrespect intended."

Rachel presented the homemade snack on Granny Mae's Currier and Ives dessert plate, garnished with fresh strawberries, a chilled glass of milk, and a delicate cloth napkin embroidered with a formal cursive letter *S*.

"None taken." Rachel was amused.

"Will you sit with me? I have so many questions about your home. And the details. I'm a researcher by profession. Questioning is in my nature."

Rachel conceded her shorter-than-normal list of chores and agreed. The guest's request was unusual. On this day, Rachel was feeling a little unusual.

On the eve of the planting of this year's crop, change was in the air. Change she needed. Change for which she longed. She could feel it.

With a hot cup of hazelnut decaf in hand, Rachel sat in the cushioned rattan chair across the room from her boisterous guest and reached for a coaster. She moved the photo on the side table ever so slightly to accommodate its placement.

"My mom calls me Sam. So should you!"

Rachel nodded. "Gladly."

"I can't tell you how much I appreciate you allowing me a few days here. I realize you were not taking bookings this week. I just want you to know I appreciate it."

Rachel nodded in an accepting gesture. "It's my pleasure!"

As Sam spoke, her eyes were drawn to the picture on the side table. A couple in formal wedding attire sat on a red tufted sofa in the middle of a grassy field.

"I love your wedding dress! Vintage becomes you!"

Rachel turned to the photo. Her heart remembered the soft breeze that afternoon at sunset and the gentle waves of hay that had surrounded them. Their love was ripe. Her body had recorded it.

"He's tall, dark, and handsome, as they say. You guys look so happy." Rachel sighed. A satisfying grin lifted her cheeks. "Yes, it was a day we'll never forget."

"I hope my stay hasn't interrupted any plans for you and…." Sam nodded her head toward the photo.

"Oh, Jackson! His name is Jackson. And no, there are… no plans." Rachel shifted the conversation from the inquiry. "More milk?"

"No, ma'am. But you can tell me about the contraption mounted on the wall behind you. It looks like there might be a story. At least I hope so!"

Sam had referenced the age-old oxen yoke. "Yes, there's a story." Rachel leaned back in her chair, looking over at the only other photo in the room. Sam followed her gaze to an ornate frame hanging on the wall.

A frail gentleman sat on the porch steps with Rachel leaning in close, her arm clasped in his. Adult children who carried the look of either the patri-arch or matriarch, or both, proudly surrounded the couple. Grandchildren were perched near their parents. The oldest was scarcely two. Sam arose and approached the photograph. She exchanged a few quick glances between the two photos—the two couples.

"Is that your family? Was the picture taken on this front porch? Is that your…husband?

Your…first husband?"

Rachel's eyes were glued to the photo. She took a deep breath, then began. "Yes, my…first husband. His name was John.

"The oxen yoke was my gift to John on the last Christmas we shared. That family photo was taken on the same day. Christmas Day. On this front porch. Our final photo."

John grew up on the farm that surrounded the house. He understood farm implements and appreciated the old ways that came before the modern conveniences he enjoyed. Though he loved the gift itself, it was the Biblical message of yokes that was Rachel's purpose in giving it.

God made a promise to Rachel when she was young. The yoke was a symbol of the promise and the life she shared with John Avery. A life of love, faith, and ultimately purpose.

"Yokes were made from a solid wooden beam and used by farmers with oxen up until the mid-nineteenth century. Then horses. Then came machinery. The yoke fit over the necks of the two oxen, joining them together. See the indentions where the yoke rubbed the neck of each animal?"

Sam reached up, moving her fingers across the worn curves. She studied the piece with great care. "My grandmother told me about this once. She was sharing a verse from her Bible. I just couldn't get a picture in my head of what she meant. Now her words make so much sense."

"Your grandmother knew the truth. Two people united in purpose and common direction can accomplish much. The work that was done by the oxen was called the *burden*. Using the yoke evenly distributed the *burden* between the two and maintained common direction.

"What a beautiful picture of relationship the way God intended! God promised that if I would commit to His ways and wait on Him, He would bless me with a husband who would walk the shared path He had chosen for us."

Rachel looked back at the photo. Her gaze locked. "That was the last Christmas on earth with my promise."

Christmas morning was always hectic. John and Rachel Avery were the first risers. They tiptoed through the house, ensuring their job as Santa's helpers had met all expectations. Then the traditional Christmas breakfast started.

Delightful aromas of French toast and baked ham would bring the family out of bed and into the gathering room.

This year, John wasn't tiptoeing through the house. His gait had changed, making his pronounced steps labored and uncertain. Double vision was permanent. Necessary steroids caused a nightmare of agitation from sounds and movement.

And the pain. The pain had taken on a life of its own. It was unrelenting. The most recent growth of the midbrain glioma brought more pain, less strength and increasing periods of confusion. The five years since the diagnosis had taken their toll.

John sat on the edge of the bed, holding his balance. "Let me help you get dressed, then we can walk together to your recliner. I'll deliver your coffee personally." Rachel made eye contact, giving John a reassuring smile and a kiss on the forehead.

"I'd like…to wear…my green plaid." His words were thick, his speech labored. "Since it's Christ-mas." As John attempted the buttons on his Christmas shirt, Rachel went ahead and plugged in the tree. It would have never been his choice to leave the day's preparations to his wife alone. It was no longer about choice.

The house was still tranquil when Rachel delivered John's coffee to the table beside his blue leather recliner. He reached out and touched her arm. "Stay." Rachel lowered herself to her knees in front of his chair. She leaned close, looking into his eyes. The white tree lights cast a calming glow on his face.

"I can't keep…my promise to you." The yuletide magic in Rachel's eyes shifted. Her heart caught in her throat.

No! Don't say it! She knew what his words meant. She wasn't prepared to hear them.

"I … I promised I wouldn't…leave you. I know now…I can't honor… that promise."

The words were spoken. Tears filled Rachel's eyes and trailed down her cheeks.

"I know. I know you can't!" She grasped John's hands and pressed them to her face. Tears gathered in his eyes.

"You have suffered more than anyone should be allowed. I'm just selfish. I want you here!" She couldn't imagine life without John. He was the kindest man she had ever known. She had never experienced love like his.

Rachel couldn't imagine that brain cancer could take him. Take their life. Their dreams. Their plans. She couldn't fathom that God would allow it.

The two lovers sat for a long period. Her head rested on his lap as his hand brushed across her hair. No words were spoken. None were needed.

Rachel shook herself from the intimate moment and stood. "I have a special gift for you!" She stepped over to the long coffee table with a cloth drape. The coffee table was a family heirloom that always sat center stage in their home. It had seen fifty years of living through the eyes of John Avery.

The massive table was constructed of rough-cut two-by-ten oak from Avery Farms. The Avery daughters grew up building tents around it, making it their stage while they put on plays, and napping underneath it. Today, it held what would be the last gift for John. One of the most meaningful of his life. Rachel removed the sheet. John knew exactly what his gift was. "A yoke!" He smiled with satisfaction.

"This symbolizes two important truths. First, that God yoked us together. He promised to send you, and he did. For that, I am forever grateful! The life we have shared has been a treasure."

"Also, in this moment, I offer this yoke to you as an encouragement of the words of Jesus that I pray will bring you comfort." Rachel flipped through the pages of John's Bible, which was resting beside his chair.

She found the Book of Matthew and moved her finger down the page to the eleventh chapter. Beginning at verse twenty-eight, she whispered the words of their Lord before him.

"Come unto me, all who are weary and burdened,
  and I will give you rest.
Take my yoke upon you and learn from me,
    for I am gentle and humble in heart,
    and you will find rest for your souls.
For my yoke is easy and my burden light."

Chapter Two

———————— ≋ ————————

It was her sophomore year. Rachel was glad to be working in the college bookstore. A little extra cash brought added security. Jobs like this were a priority for students receiving the Pell Grant. A few hours a day suited her.

From her desk in the corner of the room, she greeted one customer at a time. All that was needed was a class schedule. From a single piece of paper, Rachel rushed about the aisles of shelving to fill each order. This job gave her a degree of confidence in an unfamiliar setting. No one could start classes without first visiting the bookstore. She knew exactly what each student needed. The manager, Mrs. Davison, trusted her.

The bustle of students and faculty was beyond the door of the store. All could be observed from Rachel's perch with minimal interaction. She was comfortable there.

Rachel was attending Lane Community College along with a few thousand other students. Though in the same county, it seemed a world away from her small hometown and New Berry High School, where fellow students were more like family. Daily, she struggled with the urge to throw her hand up at bypassers, knowing many times the greeting would not be reciprocated.

Rachel's major was undeclared. Uncertain. As uncertain as her love life.

It had been years since God assured Rachel of His promise to send someone who would share her life journey. The promise remained just as relevant as it was at thirteen years old, when she first met her Savior. God had a plan for her. She believed He would be faithful to keep His promise.

The story of Ruth in the Old Testament ignited a flame in Rachel. The struggle lay in the waiting. In the waiting for her Boaz. A man who would see her. See beyond her past. Who would love and protect her as a treasure. Her past taught her that love could come much easier than a common life of purpose. She wanted both.

Opportunity came knocking often. Each attempt to take control was disastrous. Rachel's free will was proving unfriendly to God's plan. The patterns of her past were led by emotions. They shifted like sand beneath her feet.

In a gentle reminder, she heard God's loving tug within. *I am working for your good. Wait. Trust. Pray.* Rachel wrote Romans 8:28 on notecards and placed them in her house, her car, and her purse. She needed God's word before her daily. Her emotions could not be trusted. His Word could. She would serve faithfully, like Ruth, as she waited.

Lord, you have called me to your purpose and I love you. As you are working my life for good, help me in the waiting.

Rachel's beginnings were not those of the Hallmark Hall of Fame. Her mid-1960s birth had been cloaked in scandal, rejection, and secrecy. She was the living evidence of her parents' affair. Her presence was a thorn in the flesh for many.

When Rachel was still very young, her mother, Frances, accepted a marriage proposal. With two marriages and the rejection of an affair ending in heartbreak behind her, she needed a new beginning.

She was ready to forge a life for herself, her son, Pate, and Rachel. Ready to bury the unconsummated hopes and dreams that had crashed before her with Rachel's father, Buster. Love wasn't the primary emotion with the new man in her life. Security was her new motivator. It was what she chose.

Frances had been emotionally paralyzed. Yet the crippling pain of rejection was waning with time, distance, and busyness. She was finally hopeful. The hope seemed to legitimize itself as she pushed through each day.

The moving truck in the driveway represented that hope. Though Frances was moving six hours south of the only life she had known, she was ready to take the risk of a new life. She wanted a new beginning. More so, she needed it.

Frances was lovely. Natural beauty was abundant. The chestnut brunette was smart and well-spoken. In her newly rented cinderblock home of Central Florida's Pinellas Park, she was content, even excited. The Old Florida paradise was sprinkled with massive live oaks, whose branches curled down from the heights to hug the ground. Sable palms and Japanese yews added to the tropical landscape of the flamingo-hued home.

Frances accepted a job offer at the neighborhood school. A confidence she had never known began to grow. She made friends. She was valued. She was chosen.

The work at Suncrest Elementary School was a far cry from the long hours and hard labor of the hot, dimly lit shirt factory. Frances felt encouraged about her newly found career. About the way she was recreating a respectable life. A good life—children, a job, a husband, a home. And now, her blonde-haired, blue-eyed baby girl's face was not just a painful reflection of her former lover but a true blessing. A child…her child.

Rachel was not yet old enough for school. *The Florida Gazette* kept her stepfather busy in the evenings dealing with circulation. During his days, he managed the preschooler's meals, play time and nap. Frances worked in peace, knowing her baby girl was happy. And safe.

Playing freely in the backyard was Rachel's favorite activity. She danced and twirled with the clouds and sang with the birds. She loved what most five-year-old girls would. Mudpies. Butterflies. Purple Kool-Aid. Her happiness was fulfilled in her innocent world of make-believe. Rachel was happy in her new home. All was well…Then it wasn't.

Bath time in the clawfoot tub meant splashes and bubbles and giggles for Rachel. Foamy soap mountains were shaped with her petite hands and set delicately around the tub. As she twirled her body about to knock over the peaks, her eyes met someone's gaze through the crack in the bathroom door. In an instant, the eyes were gone.

Rachel turned away, then back to the door. He was there. This time, he didn't pull away. Rachel sat in the tub with her back to the door. She didn't move. She couldn't. She never had reason to doubt him…or her safety. Until now.

Each day, the scenario repeated. Rachel's fear intensified. Her little mind had no framework for what was happening. But she learned to rush through what was once a joyful childhood experience for that which was necessary.

Rachel's mother woke her with a gentle goodbye kiss. "Have a good day! Pate and I are headed out." She forced her eyes open to see her mother's face. Frances ran her fingers against the soft skin of her daughter's cheek. It felt good to Rachel. Her mother's love had been cold. Now she could feel it even on the tips of her fingers. Pate stuck his head in the door. "See you later, Dumplin!"

Rachel crawled from the bed and dressed herself in mismatched play clothes. The morning excitement for pancakes and bacon had disappeared. In its place was a submission to a turmoil that enveloped her whole being. Fear was the first to arrive when her feet found the floor. She couldn't understand her feelings. She simply knew danger was near. Mama was gone.

At naptime, Rachel skipped into the bedroom, dragging her doll by the ponytail.

She stopped short, taking a step back toward the doorway. He was there. She immediately looked away, pulling her companion to her face. Her only protector had no words and no life.

He was there on her bed. His book opened on her white chenille bedspread. He beckoned her closer. Closer to the book of pictures. To look. To touch. Curiosity led her to the bedside. Her doll was still positioned by her face, hiding the full view of his body. Rachel winced when she saw the book. When he reached for her. Her whole body shuttered.

"Shhhh. Don't tell!"

Rachel ran away. She escaped. But her young eyes had been opened, and her innocence diminished. Running away was all she could do. All she could control.

She rushed through the backyard to the shed. The door dragged. She pushed with her whole body until she could squeeze through the opening. She slammed it securely behind her.

Her tiny lungs were out of air. Her heart pounded. *Mama!*

The dark shed near the alley was her hiding place. Her refuge among the discarded furniture, cardboard boxes, and spider webs. She sat in solitude. No sound. No way to be discovered.

As Rachel stared into the darkness, a song arose in her young heart.

When I'm afraid, I'll trust in you.

I'll trust in you; I'll trust in you.

When I'm afraid, I'll trust in you.

In God, whose word I praise.

The children's Bible song from Psalm 58 had played on the church van that picked up Rachel and Pate the previous Sunday. She didn't understand it, but the words felt soothing, like a warm cloth on her face.

Bubbles and butterflies were put away. Protection was the new game. A game Rachel played alone. Naps were a thing of the past. Closed eyes meant vulnerability. Books of unclean origin had come to reside in her home. Her place of safety.

Rachel's world was forever changed by them. He was changed by them. She became prey to one whose mind was rewired by their perversion.

When Friday afternoon arrived, Rachel breathed a sigh of relief. The weekend meant safety. The weekend meant Mama and Pate. Rachel could return to playful backyard games. If only for a little while.

As evening approached, a commotion arose within the house. Rachel stopped in her tracks. Poised to hear her mother's accusation and Pate's protest. Frances was furious. "Pate! Tell me RIGHT NOW where you got this!"

The leather belt was pulled from the dresser. Punishment ensued. Pate begged his mother to stop. "I don't know where it came from! I promise!" The origin of the book of pictures was demanded.

Terror struck Rachel's heart. She realized what was happening in the house. The book. Her mother found the book. Pate was crying hysterically and screaming for his mother to stop.

Rachel knew where the book came from and to whom it really belonged. But she couldn't tell. She couldn't tell what she knew. What she had seen. What he had done. Shame rushed in. Fear took hold of her. No one could know.

Rachel climbed the chain-link fence and grabbed the branches of the holly tree, whose aged trunk was woven into the links. She scurried as high as she could. As fast as she could. The prickles and scratches on her skin gained no attention.

Rachel crouched on the highest branch, clutching the trunk. She rocked back and forth as terror settled. Her eyes were closed. She could see no one. No one could see her.

Rachel was unaware of the passing of time until the buzzing streetlight jarred her. The nightly song of the crickets had begun. Voices were quiet.

Rachel didn't understand all that transpired in the adult world of her home that night. Pate assured his baby sister. "Mama knows the truth. She made that bad man leave!" The truth of which he spoke was a different truth than Rachel's. Rachel was relieved that Frances and Pate would never know her shame. But the sadness that now loomed on her mother's face made her heart sad too.

Bubble baths became easier…with a closed door. Long afternoon naps resumed with a dozen stuffed animals circling the bed like little soldiers. Frances had not noticed the changes in her daughter. Rachel was remembering childhood, but her innocence was gone.

Summer was fleeting. It had been almost devoid of fear. Devoid of him. Caution took a front seat in Rachel's life. She was now ever-aware of her surroundings.

Pate had been visiting his father all summer. The abrupt out-of-state move to Florida had shaken him. He adored life with his father. With his beautiful half-sister, Deborah. For Pate, occasional visits were not enough. Rachel missed him. She thought often of the evening in the holly tree and the pain that had come to him because of her silence.

With a few weeks left until school started, Frances arranged for Rachel to visit Buster. Rachel didn't know her father. She had no memory of him. Of visiting his home. Being held by him.

Though he was a stranger to her, she wanted a daddy. Most little girls Rachel knew had a daddy who loved, played, and protected them. She wanted one too.

Rachel held the hand of an unknown woman, to whom Frances entrusted her. Her mother waved goodbye as the two disappeared down a long, compact corridor. The accommodating woman escorted her to the front seat of the aircraft and buckled her in. Rachel had never seen the inside of an airplane. So much was unknown for her here. And at her destination. Her timidity was intensified by her fear. The unfamiliar people. The sounds. The vibrations. The pain in her ears.

In a day, Rachel left her Florida home, visited an airport in a bustling city called Atlanta, and then arrived in the Alabama town where she was born. She had taken in a lot for an apprehensive preschooler. By evening, she had been retrieved from the airport and was sitting at a kitchen table among strangers.

The food was hot and delicious. There was limited chatter during the meal among the other children. Rachel was careful to make no mess on the lovely blue and white checkered tablecloth. She ate quietly so as to draw no attention to herself.

After the meal, she and three little girls lined up at the kitchen counter to do the dishes. From oldest to youngest, each had a job. Wash. Rinse. Dry. Put away. Respectively. Rachel dried.

After the chores were complete, the man they called Daddy pulled Rachel near his armchair. "How's your mama?" Rachel didn't expect the nervousness that emerged as he wrapped his arms around her and pulled her close. She turned her gaze downward and gave a soft response. Buster chuckled at her aversion and with a gentle touch he turned her face to his. He offered a smile. Her eyes were his eyes.

The following morning, Rachel and the other girls piled into the dated sedan with their mother. The corner grocery store clerk greeted the family and called each one by name. "Who is this little one? I don't know her." The mother looked down at Rachel. "She's a cousin from out of town." Her expressionless gaze returned to the gentleman. "She will be leaving in a few days." The clerk smiled and rubbed the top of Rachel's blonde head. "She looks a lot like your baby girl. They could be sisters."

By the end of the first full day, something had changed with Rachel's father. He was one man when she awoke. Another before she slept. In the evenings, his speech became slurred, his gait wobbly, and his words harsh and dictating.

The children worked hard in the mornings, played in the afternoons, and scurried from sight in the evenings. The little ones were certain the endings to the days were more intense due to Rachel's presence, though none knew why. Rachel could not get home to Florida fast enough. She missed Frances. She missed her familiar home. Home...where she was a daughter.

Summer turned into fall. Rachel's excitement to attend school could not be contained. She crawled into the family's Ford Fairlane next to her mother. She glanced at the seat beside her where Pate once sat. She didn't expect it to be empty this year. She wondered about his first day of school in Alabama. His first day with Deborah by his side as they boarded the yellow school bus. Did he miss her?

Rachel snuggled closer to her mother. She held her sparkly blue box with the utmost care, balanced on her lap, its contents protected. Fat pencils. Pointy crayons. Tiny scissors.

Rachel's new patent leather shoes were the shiniest she had ever seen. Her eyes didn't depart from them as Frances drove six blocks to the school. She wasn't sure what the day would hold, but in her red velveteen dress and with her beautiful mother by her side, her overwhelming pride could only mean a great beginning.

Chapter Three

––––––≋––––––

Rachel looked out over the unknown faces. Transition was again her companion. Confidence would be her greatest ally in this daunting situation. Her calf-high Old West boots accenting a ruffled-hem dress with an apron bodice didn't hinder her situation. Nor did her golden ponytails tied with baby blue ribbon.

First impressions were crucial…even in this third grade classroom.

"Girls and boys, welcome our new student. Her name is Rachel. She comes to us from Pinellas Park." Greetings of varied sincerity rang out. Some offered no greeting at all. Rachel forced a smile as her mind reeled and her heart raced.

Where is my seat? Please just let me sit down!

Two weeks earlier, Frances had remarried. She was now Frances Williams. She packed up their lives and moved to a rural trailer park a half-hour drive from Walt Disney World. Rachel had enjoyed the time with no patriarch in the home. Now they were starting over as their life patterns dictated.

Rachel's new stepfather, Martin Williams, was a heavy machine operator and union man. His skill with a backhoe provided work in the new park and a claim to fame as the operator who broke ground for the Mad Tea Party ride. Though Rachel was uncertain about the move, that fact alone impressed her.

The family of two moved into Martin's bachelor-style mobile home, which was scarcely ten feet wide. It was surrounded by a chain-link fence and citrus trees. A massive hibiscus skirted the front of the home and donned saucer-sized red blooms. The lone persimmon tree was large enough to provide nice shade, though the messiness of its fallen fruit and the yellow jackets it attracted negated the desire to utilize it. The sound of airboats on the nearby lake was a constant.

Rachel took the extra bedroom. It was just large enough to walk around the small bed and built-in dresser. She didn't care about the size. The room had a door and, most importantly, a lock.

The beginnings of this new life were good. Happiness in the honeymoon phase was euphoric, as was the usual experience. The bliss was like a fog. It concealed any possibility that happiness wouldn't last or that doom was imminent. Or that dysfunction would return and take a seat at the kitchen table.

Rachel settled in. The landscape was appealing to her country girl persona. Large open pastures with live oaks towering over low-growing palmetto. Quarter horses grazing alongside branded cattle. Osceola County was rodeos and ranches. Orange groves. Lakes and canal locks. The possibilities for adventure were endless.

Martin was good to Frances and Rachel. He worked hard on the job and at home. He was a good provider. He embraced his new life. Rachel was not sure why this kind, resourceful man had been alone.

Frances took a teacher assistant job at Rachel's school. For all the times in the family's life that poverty crept in, this was not one of them. Resources were sufficient. Even more so.

"Come on, Rachel. Let's get home and start our weekend cleaning. When Martin gets home, we're going out to dinner. We decided this morning." Frances filed the day's spelling tests and laid out resources for Monday's reading lesson. Rachel packed her book bag and threw it over her shoulder. "Can I pick the restaurant?" Her eyes sparkled with excitement.

"Absolutely! We're sure the transition over the last few weeks has not been easy. You've done a great job!" Rachel was proud of her mother's comments. To her, approval meant love. This kind of conversation was new to their family. Sharing feelings. Offering affirmations. "Thank you, Mama! I'm really trying."

On the way home, Frances and Rachel chatted, smiled, and laughed. Frances talked with Rachel, not just to her. "What do you think about cheerleading? Tryouts are in a few weeks on the school playground." Rachel beamed. "I would like to try! Karen sits next to me in class. She was a cheerleader last year. She's trying out." Rachel's life was full. She couldn't take it all in.

The chores began immediately upon their return home. Mother and daughter worked side by side, completing their work. The time for Martin's arrival came and went. Rachel's disappointment had grown as the darkness settled on the night's possibilities. She submitted to a nap on the sofa against the warmth of the folded towels.

Frances sat by the phone on the kitchen wall, her eyes outlining the designs in the wallpaper over and over as anxiety settled. No word came.

When Martin finally arrived, Rachel ran to the window. "What took him so long?" Frances was silent. She had been worried sick. Now that she could see he was fine, disgust and anger took over.

Underestimating the distance to the gate, Martin rammed it with his truck bumper. He stumbled out to lift the latch. The gate sprang open so hard that it rebounded and closed. He staggered back to the truck, cursing with every step. Acceleration through the gate left a contorted frame. When the truck stopped, he was inches from Frances' car.

"Mama! What's wrong with him? Why would he do that?" Frances put her arm around Rachel and squeezed her close. "He's drunk! Go wait in your room while I handle this." Rachel turned toward her bedroom, then turned back. "I'm hungry."

"I know, Rach. I'm so sorry. Let me handle this first." Frances turned back toward Martin's commotion in the yard. Rachel closed her door and fell onto the bed. *Is this really happening?* The fearful memories of her father's drunkenness and her life with her former stepfather came flooding back. Anger erupted in Rachel's heart. *It's ruined! It's all ruined!*

Before Rachel opened her eyes, she could feel a gnawing in her stomach. There had been no dinner. The vinyl backseat was hard and cold. Too much so for a good night's sleep. Rachel was thankful for her mother's sweater, which covered all except her chilled toes. The Ford sat alone in the church parking lot. The steeple cross cast its light onto her makeshift bed. This scenario was new.

As the first light revealed itself along the horizon, Rachel looked out, evaluating their situation. Her gaze found a lighted window near the entrance of the church. Lumens shone through the vibrant colors of the pieces of glass. A man in a robe stood leaning on a long rod. A lamb pressed in, resting against the lower portion of his leg. Rachel felt a strange warmth settle as she observed the young animal and his caregiver. She could see that he trusted the man. The hunger of her heart called out as her eyes lingered.

Rachel turned back toward her mother. Pain radiated around her neck. "A *crick*!" Granny Mae used to say. Frances was sleeping in the driver's seat, crouched against the cool glass of the closed window. In her restlessness, she cried out, "Don't leave! Please don't leave! What about our baby? Our life?

BUSTER!" The outburst frightened Rachel. She had never heard desperation in her mother's voice. Frances was frantic. Hysteria erupted as she dreamed.

Rachel reached out and touched her mother on the shoulder. She jolted awake. For a moment, Frances wasn't sure where she was. As she turned to see her daughter, she came to her senses. Pulling down the rearview mirror, she wiped tears from her face and neck and the mascara that marked her cheeks. She stared into her own eyes, frozen, wondering how she had made it so far from her beginnings.

"Are you ok, Rachel?" She maneuvered in the seat to look into her daughter's face. "I'm still hungry." Frances nodded. With a hint of desperation still on her face and holding back more tears, she smiled at her daughter's purity in this moment. "I know, Rach. I'm so sorry."

An early Saturday morning trip to the gas station restroom allowed Frances and Rachel to freshen up. Frances searched around the car for money. Her purse had been abandoned on the kitchen table. It held all her resources.

At seven o'clock, the two were sitting at the Eckerd Drug Store food counter. Frances found enough coins for grits, eggs, and toast for her baby girl. The meal served to distract Rachel from last evening's unexpected drama.

Martin had not physically hurt Rachel or Frances. But when confronted, his fist through the pantry door left evidence of his objection. In his distraction, Frances ran from the house with Rachel and drove away. For a moment, she relived the night's terror. Rachel's screams from the other room. Her rush to her mother's side, fearing injury. Their euphoria was replaced by reality.

Martin had accepted an invitation from his union buddies for a stop by the lounge the previous evening. He knew he shouldn't, but the mockery of the guys was too much. "Henpecked already! One drink won't hurt!" The truth for Martin was that one drink did hurt. He couldn't hold his liquor. Never could. Even one beer was too much. Martin was a sloppy drunk…and he got mean. Frances wasn't aware of her new husband's weakness during their short engagement. Now, it was too late.

Frances watched her daughter. She sipped her coffee and smoked her last Winston 500, found in the glove compartment. Frances' concern could not be disguised. She wasn't sure what they would encounter when the two arrived back home. Would they be safe? Should they even go home?

When Rachel had eaten the last of her grits, Frances loaded her in the car and headed to the trailer park. "Mama, I'm scared!" Frances could feel her daughter's anxiety. She felt the same.

As they drove up the dirt driveway toward the gate, Martin was there. He had attempted to repair the fence. The bends in the galvanized aluminum would always be a reminder of its previous trauma.

When Martin saw Frances and Rachel, he began to cry. "I'm so sorry! I didn't mean for this to happen. Please forgive me. I'll do anything to make it up to you." Rachel was sure it would never happen again. He was so sorry and sincere.

By the mid-seventies, Martin's union was on strike. Rachel had never seen him so frustrated. No crossing the picket lines. No working. No money. He didn't know what to do with himself.

Frances had left her job at the school after the first year. It didn't seem necessary.

In this financial crisis, the night shift at Community Care Nursing Home helped pay the bills. Frances enjoyed teaching some of the tricks of her new trade to her young daughter. "When we change your sheets on Saturday, I'll show you how to make the bed with hospital corners."

The task didn't matter to Rachel. She just wanted to spend time with her mama.

The effects of the strike were more widespread than a simple role reversal for the adults in Rachel's home. Though she experienced safety with Martin, in the absence of alcohol, fear crept in and settled. It would question every action. Every motive. It was her constant companion. The guard that filtered every circumstance.

Martin and Frances never knew of the mockery that came with their bout of lack. Rachel's snug school pants had not grown along with her nearly teenaged legs. Teasing was not easily tolerated. Necessity once again proved to be the mother of invention. Rachel took the matter into her own hands, using her mother's sewing machine and fabric remnants to add inches to her slacks. The awkward intervention was the lesser of the two embarrassments.

"When the strike is over, things will be back to normal, Rachel. I promise." Martin and Rachel ate their nightly bowl of buttered rice in silence, each missing Frances' presence.

In later weeks, as the strike ended, the union took Martin a few hours away for jobs. Due to the gas embargo and lines at the pumps, he and fellow operators carpooled. The family was thankful for the work, but carpooling put Martin at the mercy of each driver.

Friday bar stops created chaos for the family. Destruction always followed. Frances and Rachel remained familiar with the local motel.

The school bus stopped at the entrance to the trailer park. Students filed off as if it were on fire. Within what seemed like seconds, all were scattered. Except one. A girl taller than Rachel with wiry brown hair stood on the dirt road that winded through the park. Her arms were crossed with two thick textbooks tucked in. Her stance was intimidating. Rachel stared at the path in front, picking up her pace.

"Hey! I was waiting for you!" Rachel stopped. With hesitation, she turned back, trying not to make eye contact. "Yes?" The girl walked intently toward her. Rachel's heartbeat was in her ears.

"I live right over there." She gestured beyond the trailer park. "You want to come over sometime?" Rachel's shoulders relaxed. "My name is Cara Robbins." In seconds, Rachel's emotions shifted to excitement. "Sure! I'd like that! I'm Rachel."

Rachel was happy to have an escape from the sometimes turbulent homelife to which she would never become accustomed. The Robbins family made life seem easier. Even frustrations or disagreements were brief, with relationships returning to normal with ease. Rachel observed the family closely. She took it all in and learned.

They were Northerners, as were many of the neighbors. Rachel loved their Jersey accent, and they teased her deep Southern drawl. No one seemed to mind that she came from across the trailer park fence, where they sometimes spent nights in the car.

The Robbins family had migrated south to expand the family nursery business in a warmer climate. They specialized in starter plants that would be shipped out and grown elsewhere. Fifteen acres of prime Florida countryside.

There were four commercial greenhouses, with a sidewalk running through the middle of each. The golf cart could move easily from one to the other, creating efficient oversight. Sprinklers, vents, and fans. They knew their business.

The family of four was settled in their new construction built on the business property. It was more house than Rachel had ever experienced. Rachel and Cara's younger brother, Jay, shared a classroom at Jeffers Intermediate School. The three became fast friends.

Rachel would get lost in life across the fence, sometimes forgetting that she had a home, a mother, a stepfather...a past. She enjoyed the newness in her life without relinquishing her constant awareness of her surroundings or her safe distance from virtually everyone. It was the way she had been wired since the cinderblock house.

Rachel's favorite days with Cara were those spent riding horses. The quarter horses that grazed the acreage beside the greenhouses were stunning. Their gentleness took Rachel's heart and mind to a place of peace.

The three-year age difference between the girls didn't seem to matter to either. They loved their days of adventure in the still primitive Florida countryside. Cara's family took Rachel in on many weekends during the school year. In the summer, they were inseparable.

The family's attempt to move Rachel beyond her comfort zone was constant. Helping her overcome her shyness in their presence was a family goal. Though they would never learn the origin of her timidity, trust grew. Rachel loved this family that welcomed her so freely. "You're too quiet! You're too thin!" Mrs. Robbins would announce in the accent Rachel loved. Then a second helping was scooped onto her plate. She was grateful.

Whether learning rodeo tricks with the horses, playing hide and seek in the greenhouses late at night on the golf cart, or trying out a homemade raft on the shallow waters of Lake Tohopekaliga that lapped nearly to their backyards, the days were unforgettable.

Rachel was amazed at how grand life could be when she wasn't checking for danger behind every door. The Robbins family home was Rachel's sanctuary.

Chapter Four

Rachel pressed her face against the glass, tracking the white, reflective lines on the asphalt. The interstate wasn't her route of choice to get to Alabama. Frances just wanted the quickest.

It was the beautiful scenery and mom-and-pop restaurants along Highway 98's Big Bend that Rachel preferred. And the Seven-Eleven where her favorite Coke-flavored Icee was waiting. Most of their traveling was at night. Not much to see either way.

The backseat was transformed into Rachel's home away from home. Pillows and a blanket made a cozy bed. Frances' new Galaxy 500 was just the right fit for all the traveling necessities of her thirteen-year-old daughter and her favorite color of deep blue. Martin bought it brand new when the economy recovered and union work was stable. If only their family life were just as stable.

Traveling was a special event for Rachel. The trip from their Central Florida home to South Alabama was only six hours. She had enough activities for a few days. Spiral notebooks, colored pencils, stencils, and what any teenage girl needed—music. Rachel's birthday had come and gone in late

July. Her favorite gift was placed on the rear dashboard. A portable cassette player. Recordings of Rachel's favorite music were lined up side by side. Blank cassettes in abundance, ready to record family conversations.

Rachel was excited to see Aunt Ella and the cousins. And especially Pate. His full-time job, just twenty minutes from Aunt Ella's, prevented a visit to Florida. Since his graduation, he had needed all the hours that were offered to cover the responsibilities that came with his newly found independence. He would join the family in the morning. For Rachel, it couldn't come soon enough.

School was scheduled to start in a few weeks. A trip at this time was a must. After a few days away with family, Rachel and Frances would return home. New school year. New adventures with Cara.

Frances pulled down the gravel driveway at her sister's house at twelve thirty. All the lights were on. Window sashes were raised, inviting the summer breeze over worn wood and peeling paint. "Rachel! Wake up! We're here!" Rachel pulled herself from her temporary bed, leaning over the front seat. The house was just as she remembered.

Her makeshift sleeping quarters had produced an appropriately disheveled appearance from the two-hour nap. Before she could tidy herself, the screen door flew open. The relatives filed out into the damp grass.

Everyone talked at once. Patch, the family pup, yelped in sync. Aunt Ella's husband glared from behind the bedroom sheers. The full moon watched over the commotion. All while the neighbors slept.

"Rachel!" The call came through the ruckus. Rachel knew the voice. She pulled on her size sevens. Tears welled in her eyes as the laces were secured. "Ann!" The vivacious cousin leaned into the car, pulling Rachel to the yard.

In a wholehearted embrace, they rocked side to side, taking in the whole of the emotion. A quick face-to-face glance brought an outburst of laughter. "Girl, I have missed you so much!" Ann hooked her arm around Rachel's neck, pulling her close and heading toward the house. "Florida is too far away!" Their faces brimmed with the experience as chatter began.

Rachel and Ann's relationship was more like that of sisters than cousins. The two were born just five months apart. They had lived next door to each other before Rachel's move to Florida. It was the perfect scenario for two people who loved each other so much.

It would be hours before anyone slept. When the sisters and cousins reunited, there was just too much catching up to do.

Coffee was brewed. Cigarettes lit.

Adults piled on the sofa. Children gathered on the floor.

The cassette recorder was engaged.

The weekend was everything Rachel had hoped for. Family meals, old stories, and much laughter.

Being near Pate for a few hours warmed her heart. Seeing with her own eyes that he was doing well pacified her. *Pate, can you ever forgive me for the secret of the cinderblock house?* Could Rachel ever forgive herself?

Before the sun descended on the day, everything shifted for Ann and Rachel. "Rachel, please don't go! Stay here! We could share my room. Go to school together. Go to church together." Rachel didn't even think. She heard her answer the same time Ann did.

The two converged on their mothers. Asking. Pleading. Laughing. Impulsivity was not uncommon in their world. It was addictive, as was the initial change it created.

All agreed. It was done.

Frances and Rachel agreed to attend Sunday morning service with Ann before Frances' departure. As songs of worship were sung, quiet tears flowed down Frances' face. As the pastor spoke, a steady stream remained. God held her. He knew the hurt that kept her at bay. The pain she carried. He remembered the little girl who surrendered to Him years before her young world was shattered. Before everything seemed lost. Before she began cycles of destruction. He loved her too.

Monday morning arrived. Arrangements were made. Frances drove away, contemplating the cycle to which she returned and the courage Rachel had to step away. For Frances, there were still decisions to be made.

The place Rachel visited was now her home. Aunt Ella went off to work, leaving Ann and her younger brothers to fill the final days of summer. And now Rachel. Ann's stepfather's presence was scarce every day.

Rachel barely had her feet on the floor before Ann was making the bed. Chores awaited the only daughter. Now Rachel was by her side. As they darted through the rooms of the small house, the laundry basket filled up.

Cold scrambled eggs and toasts were waiting on the kitchen table. The girls enjoyed a few quiet moments of breakfast before the boys awoke. Then the two were off to the laundromat to start the loads from the weekend.

The washer and dryer worked their magic. The girls sat on the tall counter meant for folding. Through the hum of the appliances, they talked of boys, eighth grade, and the student crusade at Ann's church the next week. "Rachel, I can't wait for you to be a part of the crusade. I want you to learn about Jesus." Rachel was unsure what it all meant. She just wanted to be with Ann.

With the quarters Aunt Ella left next to the plate of eggs, the girls shopped at the downtown Piggly Wiggly. It was among a dozen businesses that lined the main street of the small town. A can of chicken noodle soup would be a summer lunch shared among the children.

The first week as a guest in Aunt Ella's home had passed. Ann and Rachel looked forward to the coming Saturday morning with no chores. The girls snuggled in their double bed with the August breeze floating over their pillows.

Rachel's dreams were tumultuous. Arguments. Discord. She opened one eye to see the white sheer dancing in the summer breeze. Crickets were singing in the distance. She snuggled deeper.

Voices erupted. It was not a dream. Aunt Ella and her husband had returned from their night on the town. Full of spirits and frustration, a heated argument ensued. In an instant, Rachel's mind revisited her tiny trailer bedroom. The panic. But this night was different. There were more than words and sounds. The night was full of screams. Accusations. Breaking glass. Then a thunderous crash.

Rachel jumped from Ann's double bed and ran to the adults' bedroom door. Pushing and beating on the locked door, she pleaded. Aunt Ella was crying. "Stop hurting her! Let me in!" Rachel was desperate.

"Go back to bed, Rachel. I'll be…fine." Aunt Ella's tone was quiet and weak. Her voice was low to the ground, where the crash had sounded. Where the wall shook. He was now silent.

Rachel's mind raced. "I'm going to run to the police station and get help!"

"No, Rachel! That will only make it worse. Please go back to bed!"

Rachel felt a hand on her arm. A gentle voice spoke through the darkness. "Come back to bed, Rachel. If we try to stop him, it will only get worse. Please trust me."

Disbelief set in. *Who would pick up Aunt Ella? Who would take care of her wounds? Who would make him pay?*

Ann held Rachel's hand as they returned to their room. With every step, Ann prayed for her mother. For her safety, her healing, and her salvation. The night fell silent. Hopelessness settled over the house like the stifling August heat as the breeze subsided. Another family secret was kept.

As morning broke, Rachel awoke to the movement of the adults readying themselves for the day. Their conversations were as normal as ever. Not a harsh word was spoken.

Rachel didn't venture from the bed. She peered through the slight opening in the door from the safety of the covers. Aunt Ella looked beautiful as usual. Through the sheer sleeves of her blouse lay the evening's punishment. Muted blues and blacks extended from shoulder to wrist.

Last night was not a dream. Aunt Ella was wearing reality.

Through the thicket at the edge of the yard, Ann and Rachel made a path. The girls found solace in the clearing. In this quiet place, there was peace. The Saturday afternoon sun filtered through the branches of the dogwood, whose blooms had come and gone in the spring. Ann recounted the story of the red tinge on the edges of its white flowers. How it signified the cross and the blood of Jesus shed for the sins of all mankind. Rachel tried to imagine it.

The cousins lay on their backs. Side by side. Gazing into the perfect creation and resting in the gentle movement of the leaves in the breeze. Random rays reached the mossy grass where the blanket had settled. In this place, there was no cooking. No cleaning. No laundry. No screams. Just two girls. Cousins.

The girls rushed about the bedroom getting ready for church. The student crusade was scheduled to begin at six. Rachel was excited. As Ann had shared about God over the previous week, a hunger grew. She wanted to know more.

Who was this man called Jesus? Rachel's thoughts wandered back to her childhood. Each man she encountered eventually brought pain, fear, and rejection. *Would He be different?* There was a battle within that Rachel could not articulate. But she was compelled to seek Him out.

Rachel sang and laughed and listened in the sanctuary. Every presentation of the evening was woven with threads of the man, Jesus. Every prayer, every skit, every song, and every verse were imprinted on her scarred heart.

In an instant, Rachel's mind was transported back to the clearing. She could see the leaves of the trees as she lay on the blanket, the wind softly moving them about.

Rachel. A whisper came from within her. *It is my Spirit who moves your heart tonight. Like the wind that you cannot see moves the leaves.*

The faces of men began to flood toward her. Each with the damage brought to her mind. To her heart. Her body. Her life. Fear stood guard.

The sixteenth verse of the third chapter of the book of John was recited from the pulpit. "Jesus is here tonight. He died for you. He wants to be your Lord and Savior. Will you open your heart to let Him in? He loves you!" When the word *love* reached Rachel's ears, every sound and every movement began to slow around her. She could no longer hear the piano or the words spoken from the platform.

Love? You love…me? You really…love me! Rachel knew love in that moment. Miraculously. Completely. She could feel it in every cell of her body. She closed her eyes to take it all in. To hold herself there. It was a moment of perfect love. *Yes! Yes! Come into my heart and live! Jesus, let my heart be your home.*

Warm tears flowed down Rachel's cheeks. Her little hands moved from her side and began to lift upward. This was the purest reality she had ever known. She surrendered to the one man whose perfect love cast away her fear.

That warm August night on a green tweed pew, the course of Rachel's life was changed. One moment. One decision. A new life had been born from disappointment.

The school year began. The work that accompanied it was necessary. But it was a different learning that took center stage. Ann began to disciple Rachel, along with their neighbor and friend, Tina. Each evening, the Holly Hobby bedspread held their Bibles, devotionals, and journals.

Chapters were read, Scriptures memorized, and Bible songs of worship sung. "I have hidden your word in my heart that I might not sin against you." Ann encouraged them by reading aloud from Psalm 119. "The Spirit of him who raised Jesus from the dead is living in us. Romans 8:11 tells us this. Now, we must let the Word of God renew our minds." Rachel and Tina listened and learned.

By mid-September, Frances had returned to New Berry with a small U-Haul in tow. It held everything she and Rachel owned. She knew leaving Martin was imminent. It took longer for her courage to catch up to her decision. His promises had lost their luster many Fridays ago.

Frances and Rachel were thankful for Aunt Ella's kindness and hospitality, but Rachel longed for her mother's return. Now the two were together again. Fight-or-flight would no longer be the norm. Their home could be a place of peace.

It didn't take long for Rachel to settle into her new room. The little rental home was old. Not in a chic way. Just old. Faux brick siding wrapped the exterior. The windows were neither plumb nor level. The wind sought out every crack.

Light sockets on a single cord hung from the ceiling in each room. Pull for on. Pull for off. The swaying bulbs cast their shadows, concealing years of neglect. The home portrayed their current state of poverty. In their lack, they were satisfied.

Frances' cycles of life were not easily abandoned. Within a few weeks, she was introduced to a local gentleman who was immediately mesmerized by her unmatched beauty, her intelligence, and her sense of humor. Thomas Stein seemed to be a kind man. At the onset, most men seemed kind.

Frances welcomed the attention. *New beginnings* were her drug of choice. She craved the high. To be chosen. To be sought-after and desired. Not out of selfishness. It was simply the way her life experiences shaped her.

Rachel was not taking the bait. Not this time. She kept her distance. She maintained a stern, disagreeable countenance to ensure Thomas knew he was unwelcome. That his gestures wouldn't fool her.

Rachel was surprised when Thomas invited her on his first date with Frances. He never thought to leave her out. This was new for Rachel. It was unusual for Frances.

The racetrack was exhilarating. It was loud and busy and exciting. The smell of burning rubber dominated the air. Rachel could smell it even in her hair. Thomas spoiled the two. He offered his guests the whole experience. Hot dogs, popcorn, and Coca-Cola. And a black and white checkered flag for Rachel. He accompanied her to the pit as each driver signed her souvenir.

Rachel enjoyed the evening, but she maintained her disapproval with her frown, her distance, and her silence. She watched Thomas' every move. A dread lurked. The trauma of Rachel's short life brought fearful anticipation that arose involuntarily. An unrelenting foe.

Thomas and Frances became good friends. Then more than friends. Thomas fell in love with Frances...and Rachel.

As winter approached, Rachel found that her heart was softening. She didn't expect it. She didn't want it. Despite all her protests, her protective walls were coming down.

Thomas taught Rachel to drive on the back roads. Frances objected, but he reassured her. He taught her about the old ways of living. Growing sugar cane. Milling it into syrup. Making biscuits. Cornbread. Cooking peas. He conveyed an appreciation for antiquated artifacts that were still a part of his daily life. He even taught her to operate the asphalt roller used by his company, Stein Paving. "Don't be afraid. I'm right here. I won't let anything happen to you."

Rachel's anger and fear subsided. Thomas showed his love every day. Rachel realized that she loved him too. For the first time in her life, Rachel knew what the love of a father looked and felt like. She was loved. And safe. Love and safety had never existed together in her world.

At Christmas, Frances had a ring on her finger. A wedding was scheduled for Valentine's Day.

Gifts were abundant and meaningful. The three joined Thomas' family for Christmas dinner. The season felt as perfect as Rachel thought possible. The icing…a little house downtown New Berry purchased for the family to be. The remodel began. Rachel was all in.

Rachel welcomed the three-day January weekend. The wedding day was just one month away. She dreamed of her new home. New father. New life. All her defenses were down. She embraced all the good things life was sharing.

When she arrived home from school, Frances was loading her suitcase into the car. "Rachel, pack a bag. Just enough for the weekend." She walked back into the house with no explanation. Rachel followed.

"Where are we going? I thought we were working on the new house this weekend." Frances paused. "I can't go through with it, Rachel. I have to get away from this place. Martin invited us to visit him this weekend."

Rachel stood frozen in disbelief. Her body began to tremble as anger arose. "Please tell me you're not doing this! Does Thomas know?" Frances turned away. "He'll know soon enough."

Tears of anger and disappointment collided in an uncontrollable outburst. "What is wrong with you? How can you do this? I'm finally happy! I thought WE were happy!" Frances stared. No expression emerged. "Get your clothes. We're leaving in ten minutes."

With obstinacy, Rachel sat on the sofa and crossed her arms. Frances hesitated for several seconds, then pulled seven one-dollar bills from her purse. Placing them on the coffee table, she gave a last glance at Rachel, then turned and walked away. All they had become was now undone.

As night fell on the old house, Rachel rehearsed the afternoon in her head. She knew her life had taken a turn from which she would never return. She was thankful Thomas slept one more evening with his dreams intact. For she knew that with the rising sun, she would become the adult and he the child.

Chapter Five

———————≈———————

John Avery was a farm boy. His tan, slender frame topped out at six feet. Sun-kissed highlights accented the blond waves on his barbershop haircut. The highlights came naturally from hours spent on the old Massey Ferguson as he helped tend the 250 acres of Avery Farms.

John's cowboy boots were worn. Certainly not for show. They were necessary for the days of hard farm labor. And convenient for rounding up stray cattle that ventured through the fence to Indigo Creek, bordering the farm to the west. The cowhide on his size twelves had recorded each step.

John boasted a 10-inch scar that extended from hip to knee. It was the topic of much teenage-boy banter around New Berry. As a rambunctious six-year-old, he had stepped across the rarely used dirt road that ran through the family property with such confidence that he hadn't noticed the soldier's moving sports car. He had been catapulted into the blackberry bushes that lined the clay banks of the narrow road. The dust settled, and John found himself in a hospital bed with Mr. and Mrs. Avery by his side.

Pastor Jenkins stood over the family and offered a prayer. A frightened soldier paced in the waiting room. John's older sister, Kaye, sat beside him with a book in hand. As John was wheeled into surgery, Daddy put on a brave face. Mama cried.

A metal rod inserted into John's femur would ensure the healing of the bone. The remaining scar had become the badge of honor of a self-proclaimed rogue country boy. New Berry's finest. In reality, John was shy to a fault. But in his element, he was an All-American boy living the dream. A tractor. A truck. A horse. A dog. In his free time, he and Scout would trot off into the woods with Smokey, his Australian collie, not far behind. Alone didn't mean lonely. John preferred it.

John was handsome with captivating hazel eyes. Dating and socializing could have been the norm. Not for him. His weekend nights were spent sprawled in the recliner. A large pepperoni pizza and the latest episode of *BJ and the Bear* were his companions. His date night. He was satisfied with homelife and work. For now.

Farm days were long. There was no envy of John's father's claim on the newer Ford with a cab that provided protection from the elements. John respected his elder and knew one day he would have a tractor of his choosing. Sunday afternoons were spent gazing through the fence of the local farm equipment dealership, daydreaming of just that.

John had stewarded his savings account with precision since he was twelve years old. He had great pride in paying cash for his first car at sixteen. One more harvest would seal the deal on a new tractor.

March approached along with John's eighteenth birthday. Mr. Avery invited his only son for a walk over the east ridge. He placed his hands squarely on John's shoulders and made a proposition. "Son, graduation is just a few months out. Soon, New Berry High School will be in your past. It's time for you to decide about your future."

"If you want to go to college, we will make it happen." Mr. Avery's speech slowed. His tone lowered. "However, if the life we have on this farm is what you want, I want to offer you a partnership." John spent the last decade matching steps with his dad in the daily ins and outs of the family business. Mr. Avery knew he deserved this opportunity and was ready for it.

For John, there was really no question—no competition. His earliest memories were of driving the tractor on tiptoe, stretching to see over the steering wheel. Sunshine on his skin. Grease on his jeans. Diesel fumes in his hair. Living off the land was all he had ever known. All he ever wanted. And if truth be told, Mr. Avery wasn't just John's father and boss. He was his best friend.

"Ok, Dad! I'm in! I want to continue the tradition."

Each man extended his right hand with resolve to seal the deal, making a deal the way *real men* did. Mr. Avery threw his arms around his son, who was a full two inches taller, hugging with such strength that John was lifted off the ground. "A handshake and a prayer! Good times ahead, son!" It was destiny.

The Averys came from a long line of farmers. When John was born, his father and grandfather were partners. As the United States military expanded flight training at the nearby Fort Redding Army Base, the government completed a land buyout to build a heliport. Their choice was prime property that made up the Averys' generational legacy. Flight training fields began to dot the once-quiet countryside.

Mr. Avery, the younger, with his wife, daughter, and one-year-old son in tow, purchased his own acreage and relocated five miles to the west in the same county. John grew up on the heels of his father, who toiled to make a living. Just as his own father and grandfather before him. They set out with great expectations and dedication to their task.

Though fate had not yet spoken.

Planting went well for the partners. In record time, crops broke through the soil and made a good stand. The rain would take them to the next level and move them past crucial plant development.

But the rains never came. Drought was a word no farmer wanted to hear. No one could have predicted the disaster. Fear replaced excitement and expectation for small family farms built on generations of sweat.

The men held the reins of the business close to get through the season. This wasn't the first year of struggle, and it wouldn't be the last. Crop insurance and irrigation became topics of discussion at the dinner table. Mrs. Avery might have been concerned, but it never showed. Rain or shine, she made sure the family had a hot meal three times a day.

Meals were not from the grocery store. Meals came out of the freezer, from the canning shelf, or directly from the garden. Mrs. Avery and Kaye spent their summers picking, shelling, shucking, canning, and preparing meals while the men tended the livestock and the crops. Everyone had a part to play.

"We need to protect against droughts of the future." Mr. Avery laid out the plan. "Ensure that water will be there for the crops. We can dig a pond in the lowland where the springs erupt. And add irrigation. We'll be able to pump as much water out as needed. It'll be expensive, but sometimes you need to spend money to make money."

Mr. Avery was a smart businessman as well as a skilled farmer. John trusted his father. He knew he was right. The natural springs would prove to be the lifeblood of future crops. The development of a pond began in the ravine where the spring waters gathered.

The year was harder work than either man imagined. A six-acre pond was dug with machinery and manpower. *Sweat of the brow* took on new meaning for the two and their farmhand, Luke. The toll of hard back labor made neck traction a nightly affair for Mr. Avery.

In hindsight, the year of drought was a blessing in disguise. New ways for a new time. The drought had thrust the Averys into newer ways of agriculture. It was the early eighties. Interest rates were high. The expansion loan would be repaid annually as crops were sold in the fall of the year. The farm itself served as collateral. The pond was dug. Irrigation installed. After months of backbreaking work, their future was secure.

Most days, John was a reddish hue from head to toe. Clay dust settled in his ears, his pockets, and even piled up at the top of his boots. Breaking land and starting a new year of planting was a dirty job. He loved it. John switched to his father's tractor. The cab was certainly a luxury. He turned the radio to his favorite country station and engaged full throttle. Nothing could hinder him in this place. He and the land were one.

Mr. Avery hadn't been out of the house for five days. A virus of sorts, they were sure.

Lord, help my dad. He wants to work. He needs to work. John had never needed the power of prayer like he did at this moment in his life. Now it seemed it was all he had.

John knew Jesus was the source of his help. He first met Him at Vacation Bible School at Rocky Head Church, where he had marked a pew since he was just a toddler. The annual ritual was as much a social event as a spiritual encounter. He, along with other fifth-grade boys, stood side by side, lining a pew.

John was still sweaty from the round of freeze tag played before the closing assembly in the sanctuary. The knees of his jeans were embedded with dirt from the game, and a purple ring stained his lips from the night's refreshments. He was ready for the *amen*, then a few more minutes of outdoor play would close down VBS for the year.

John had heard the pastor share the Gospel of Jesus Christ many times. On this night, it all seemed new. There was no emotional tug. John simply knew he was ready to accept the Jesus Pastor Jenkins shared. To believe.

John prayed along with others who answered the call. The decision was made. He could feel a joy and an assurance that Jesus would be a friend who would stick closer than a brother. Through thick and thin. He had seen his father walk with Jesus daily. Now they could walk together.

John finished laboring in the field for the day. He was beat. Cows still needed a check. He couldn't go another day without putting his eyes on the herd. The new calves. The expectant mothers. The coyotes were never far away. Lying in wait for any opportunity. Every resource on the farm needed protection.

A prayer of thanks was lifted as John drove away from the pasture. *All is well. Thank you, Lord!* He headed to the hog barns. It seemed the truck knew the way without John's help. Morning and night. Clock work. Then home to a hot shower and a late dinner.

John was up early, making a mental list. Mr. Avery wasn't at the table when John sat down. He struggled to remember a time when his father wasn't already at the table, teasing Mama. Making her blush. Bragging on her cooking.

Chatter over homemade biscuits with Mama's blackberry jelly was common. The men laid out the plans for the day and divvied up the work. Mama rarely sat. She stood at the stove to finish second helpings of eggs, sausage processed from last winter's hog, or whatever abundance God had provided. No food was touched until thanks was given.

Today, the kitchen was quiet. "How was the night, Mama?" Mrs. Avery pulled a jar of her jelly from the cabinet and added it to the table near the cast iron skillet of biscuits.

"It was a long night. I'm not sure he slept at all. I hope he will be able to eat something today." She said no more. The creases along her forehead and the absence of a smile were more telling than words.

John heard his father call from the back of the house. He left his second helping and hurried to the bedroom. "Stay at the door, son! I don't want you catching this stuff. One of us must be in the field."

John stood on the threshold, leaning on the door frame. He scanned his father's face as he spoke. It was pale and had begun to thin in the few days since the virus came. "Keep prepping for the peanuts. They're our future." Mr. Avery made eye contact with his only son and nodded affirmatively. "You know what to do."

Peanuts were the main crop of Avery Farms. Cotton was once the crop of choice. A powerful moneymaker that saturated the market in the region. Just one season in the past significantly changed agriculture in the South. More than seven decades earlier, an enemy of the farmer and the economy swept through, destroying the blooms and buds of cotton plants. The devastation of the boll weevil.

What the enemy meant for evil, the Lord will use for good! Folks in the Bible Belt would not be done in. The boll weevil's wrath forced farmers to diversify from an exclusive cotton crop. Peanut farming became an essential way of life. Prosperity followed.

Peanut prices were protected with government subsidies. For that, the Averys were thankful. Hog prices could bottom out. As they often did. Fuel and fertilizer costs could skyrocket. "If the Farm Bill continues to give price guarantees, peanut farming will endure. We can stay afloat." Mr. Avery was confident.

Months passed. The summer maintenance of crops and livestock brought a reprieve for John. The peanuts grew. Livestock multiplied. As fall approached, anxiety began to build over the harvest. He and Luke would struggle to bring in the peanuts alone.

Mr. Avery was homebound. After his flu-like symptoms didn't resolve, there was testing for other culprits. He was now undergoing treatment for hepatitis. "It will take a few months for full recovery," predicted the doctor. If resolution was coming, it was slow. John had his doubts.

As John surveyed the peanuts, he saw a dust trail over the ridge. It was Mr. Avery's farm truck. He was relieved that his dad was feeling well enough to get out of the house. The door opened. To John's surprise, it was Mrs. Avery. "I need you at the house!"

The two rallied at the barn. Her concern couldn't be hidden. Her voice trembled. "The abdominal pain is getting worse. Your dad needs to go to the hospital."

In less than one hour, the Avery family of four was sitting in the emergency waiting room of Health Center South. The facility was forty miles south of their home. John had driven it in twenty-five minutes flat.

HCS was a public hospital. No one could be turned away. The waiting room was packed. Mrs. Avery held their health insurance card in hand, as a middle-classman would. Whether a *have* or a *have not*, they all waited together for their name to be called.

Mr. Avery bent over in pain. It was the worst he had experienced so far. Sitting up was difficult. "I can't find a comfortable position. I need something for pain!"

A nurse stepped out from the triage area and called for Mr. Avery. He couldn't walk. John lifted his father with great care. He followed his mother through the door to a bed surrounded by a curtain. Then he returned to the waiting room, where he and Kaye sat in silence.

It was a few hours before Mrs. Avery emerged from the back. She was alone. Her face was worn. "They're keeping your daddy. There is finally some relief from the pain. He's been sleeping.

"The doctor is lining up some tests. Here's a list of what I need you to bring from home." John gave his mother a long, tight hug. "It's not good, John. Hold down the fort. I'm not going to leave his side." With a kiss on her daughter's forehead, she disappeared.

John found himself sitting in the back pew of First Community Church. *God, what are we going to do?* The tests had come back with the worst possible answers. Hepatitis was a misdiagnosis.

In one year, everything had spiraled downhill. Drought. Debt. Now disease.

Mr. Avery had always been strong, decisive, and the rock of the family. Now, the man who was a part of almost every memory of John's life was dying.

Chapter Six

━━━━━ ≈ ━━━━━

The piano and organ in concert cued the congregation. Hymnals were poised. Parishioners in appropriate stance. The proclamation rang out through the sanctuary in song.

Great is Thy faithfulness.

Great is Thy faithfulness.

Morning by morning new mercies I see.

All I have needed thy hand hath provided.

Great is Thy faithfulness, Lord, unto me.

The verses pierced Rachel's heart. She could never help but respond when the Spirit of God moved her. *Thank you, Lord, for your faithfulness! I don't know why you love me. But I'm so glad you do.*

Rachel had found contentment in waiting for God to reveal His plan. She was learning that as she truly trusted Him with the results, a peace settled deep inside. A peace described in Philippians 4:7. The kind beyond understanding. She was amazed at how much space was freed up in her mind when she stopped wondering when and how God would answer her prayer.

As the verses ended, the musicians played on. The choir was dismissed and filed out of the loft as the congregation greeted one another. The sanctuary overflowed with joyful conversations, affirmations, laughter, and hugs.

Rachel smiled out over the sweet commotion among the congregation. As her eyes scanned, there he was on the back row. John Avery. She wondered what brought him to First Community Church today. His family attended a church near their farm.

Rachel made her way to the back. "Hi John! It's good to see you. It's been a while. High school maybe?" John barely made eye contact before his gaze dropped to the floor. "Yeah, I think we shared a phys. ed. class when I was a senior."

Rachel giggled. "You're right. Seniors and freshman in the same PE class. I'll never forget. Dodgeball Fridays scarred me for life. I'm not sure who thought THAT was a good idea." John laughed just enough to break his smile. "What have you been up to since high school? Didn't I see you in Barton Hardware once?"

"I'm in my second year of college. Just plugging along. Hoping I can figure out what I want to be when I grow up," Rachel shared as John's intrigue increased. "And yes, I work in the hardware store twice a week. Miss Barton and I have a deal. I work two days a week in the store and help her with house cleaning in exchange for a few rooms."

She paused to see if John had anything else to say. His look was suddenly serious. Rachel remembered his shyness. "It's good to have you here today, John. I hope you'll come again." She extended her hand.

John gently took hold of Rachel's fingers. He lifted his eyes to hers and straightened his posture. "I'm sure I will." His voice was gentle. Rachel swallowed hard. She felt the touch send shivers through her body. As she turned to walk away, she tilted her head upward and smiled. "Well, well, well, Lord. Look at that!"

When the congregation settled, Pastor Stephens took the pulpit. "I want to share a special prayer request before the sermon. Most of you know John Avery, Sr. He and his family need our prayers. He has been diagnosed with late-stage colon cancer."

Quietness fell over the room. Rachel looked back at John. His head was in his hands.

Lord, help them! Cancer. It was so rare. Rachel's heart broke for John. For his family.

She knew the trauma that came with family illness. Emphysema had taken her mother a few years earlier. Her stepfather, Martin, had died months later. Lung cancer. A lifetime of chain smoking had literally taken the breath from their lungs. Rachel was thankful for the restoration between the two when Martin relinquished drinking. Their home became a place of peace. A place for which Frances longed. Hearing Pastor Stephen's announcement reminded Rachel of the devastation of disease in her own family. Her heart ached for the Averys.

When the service ended, a circle developed around John. Support and prayers were offered. John, Sr. was well known and well loved. Everyone was in shock.

Rachel tried to maneuver around the crowd heading for the door. A hand touched her arm. "Hi, Rach!" She turned to see Mr. Browning, or Uncle Jimmy, as he was affectionately called by one and all. Rachel grabbed him around the neck and squeezed him. "Hi handsome! How's my favorite farmer?"

"Did anybody ever tell you that you have pretty eyes?" Rachel laughed out loud. She directed a confirming nod toward the older gentleman. "Only you, Uncle Jimmy! Only you!"

He took a quarter out of his pocket. Taking Rachel's hand in his, he placed the coin in her palm, closing her fingers around it. "For the college fund." She grinned. This was their little tradition. Pretty eyes. College fund.

Jimmy Browning was a kind, gentle man. He always made Rachel smile. He was a local farmer. Salt of the earth. Always willing to serve and lend a helping hand. He would have been a great father.

"I want you to meet a friend from Gainesville, Georgia." Jimmy threw his hand in the air, motioning the young man toward them. "Jackson, over here!" He approached and extended his hand to Rachel. "Good afternoon. Jackson Stone, ma'am." He nodded politely toward her.

His deep Southern voice caught Rachel off guard. He towered over the congregation. His blue eyes were piercing against his tanned skin. Soft curls moved in and out of his collar as he turned his head.

"Jackson is studying civil engineering at UGA. He's going to build bridges." Jackson blushed. "We'll see Uncle Jimmy. Right now, I'm just hoping to make it out of Advanced Structural Dynamics this semester. Lots of prayer happening in my life." He chuckled.

"Jackson, what brings you to Alabama?" Rachel inquired as she looked over her shoulder toward the still-crowded area around John. "It's fall break. I like to come down in the spring and fall to help Uncle Jimmy with some of the planting and harvesting.

"Keeps me right with God, he says." Uncle Jimmy nodded and gave a thumbs up. "I'll be here for a few weeks."

"It was nice to meet you. Come back anytime." The two exchanged nods. Rachel gave a playful wink to Uncle Jimmy.

As she turned toward the exit, she paused, glancing toward John. He looked up, catching her gaze. "I'm so sorry," she mouthed from across the room. He nodded, accepting her sentiment.

Rachel pulled the den drapes shut for her Sunday afternoon nap. She settled on the sofa, embracing her crocheted afghan. Naps came easily for Rachel.

Usually. She couldn't shake the news about John's dad. He was heartbroken for sure. A genuine, kind-hearted guy.

Before her eyes were even closed, the phone rang. "Hi Rachel. This is Angela White.

I saw you chatting with John Avery today at church. My family asked him to accompany us today. Just to give him a little while away from the sadness of his father's diagnosis. I have a question." Angela paused. "I was wondering if you might…consider going out with him? Friday night?"

Rachel contemplated briefly. She didn't feel surprised or even uneasy about the call. She felt completely at peace about the question. And her response. "Yes. I would like that!" Angela shouted over the phone, "Great! John has been a homebody too long!" It was time for change.

"I'll pick you up on Friday at 6 p.m. John will meet us at New Berry Stadium."

Friday night football brought a community together. At a late September home game, nearly every member of New Berry could be found. The bleachers were always packed. Except for tonight, with four feet of reserved seating, Angela White had marked for two guests. John and Rachel. A divine appointment.

John hooked the last wagon of peanuts to the one-ton truck. It was a heaping load. The last acres of the day were the best so far. The vines had been loaded.

He was happy about the abundance, but at the forefront of his mind was the five-foot-four blonde who would be waiting at the high school. He hated to be late to the game. He had explained his plight to Angela. "The crops have to come first."

John and Luke had taken on the entire workload for Avery Farms. Mr. Avery hadn't worked in several months. Not since a few days after the onset of his symptoms.

Darkness had come, and a heavy dew was settling over the land. John pulled the wagon under the pole barn. A large duct was hooked to the back of the wagon and a motor engaged. Hot air began to blow through the peanuts. A steady roar overtook the silence of the countryside.

John rushed to the metal shower in the laundry room. He was hardly suitable to go through the house to the main bathroom with its pink tile and ruffled curtain. He was thankful for a hot shower that removed all evidence of the day. His favorite Levi's, a plaid Western shirt with snaps instead of buttons, and a perfect white t-shirt hung on the back of the door. *Mama!*

Bell Avery was a quiet woman. Mrs. Bell, as her husband called her. John took quietness from her, for sure. She worked from dawn to dusk. Then some more. She was often seen at the clothesline in bare feet, hanging the laundry. A perpetual task.

She had house dresses for casual homelife and smart dresses for town, church, and visiting with neighbors or kin. Pants were never worn. It just wasn't done.

She cared for her family very well. Their needs always came before her own. The ironing board was a constant in the den. "As long as I'm able, you're going to look like you have a mama who cares!" No one minced words with Mrs. Avery about this. She wouldn't have it.

John exited the laundry room into the den, where his parents were watching television. Mr. Avery was propped among pillows for the greatest degree of comfort. He had lost fifty pounds since this journey began. Mrs. Avery matched socks.

John was dressed to a tee, his blond, sun-kissed highlights all in place. With more Old Spice than he had ever attempted.

"Dad, the last load I pulled to the drying barn looks great! I think we're going to clear two tons per acre in that field. I've never seen anything like it!" Mr. Avery lifted his head and turned toward his son. He watched as he hurriedly returned his wallet and keys to his pockets.

The excitement in John's voice was a little more than Mr. Avery was accustomed. He was convinced it was not about peanuts and poundage. "I'm glad to hear it, son. How's that truck of yours looking? Is it suitable for a young lady?"

John paused. He never made eye contact. "I washed it and cleaned it out last night."

"Good! Now get out of here and go have some fun!" John was relieved to hear his father's encouragement. He had struggled with the pursuit of happiness in his own life when his father's life was a constant struggle. He hugged his dad and kissed his mother on the cheek. She giggled when their eyes met.

Mr. Avery believed in the sovereignty of God. He knew the days God had written down for his life were now in the double digits. He needed to know his boy would be alright. He wanted John to find a woman to share his life. *Lord, this is all up to you. Do what only you can do.*

John followed the road to the bright lights. He rarely attended football games. He was the star player in a different field each fall. Vehicles lined the roadsides. Overflow from the bumper-to-bumper parking lots. John pulled his four-wheel drive over the curb between a few trees at the edge of the school campus.

He paid his admission and headed toward the rendezvous point. All along the way, high school buddies greeted him. Community folk stopped him to ask about Mr. Avery. He was too polite not to pause to answer. All the while, he glanced toward the bleachers, looking for her.

The first half had ended. Football fans moved about. John stood at the bottom of the bleachers, scanning.

There she was.

Rachel saw him just as he spotted her. She smiled. His face flushed. He took a deep breath and started climbing. The two settled in with minimal discussion. Kaye, who was two years older than John, teased him from a distance. As a sister would. She had never seen her little brother on a real date. Not like tonight. She couldn't resist looking back. He refused to make eye contact with her.

The couple was relieved when the game finally ended. There were too many eyes watching. As the two maneuvered through the post-game crowd, John took Rachel's hand, boring a path for their escape. He opened the truck door, gently supporting her arm as she found her spot. Ensuring she was tucked in appropriately. A satisfying grin made its way to Rachel's cheeks… where it would remain.

"Rachel, do you mind if I run by the farm on our way to town? I need to check a peanut dryer." Rachel gave a confusing look. "Peanut dryer?" John laughed. "I'm sure that sounds strange. I need to get the percentage of moisture down before I can take the peanuts to the buying point. Since you live at Mrs. Barton's, you have probably heard the low roar of Jimmy Browning's dryers during the fall nights. That's life in the country!"

The farm talk intrigued Rachel. She was a country girl at heart. Memories of her life in the trailer park—the greenhouses, horses, and cattle—flooded her mind…as did those of her dear friend, Cara.

The late hour left fast food as their only dinner option. John waited for Rachel to choose her preference, then gladly drove to Wendy's. The lobby was so cold that the windows fogged.

John could see Rachel shivering as she tried to eat. He could even hear a quiver in her voice. He excused himself and returned shortly with a jacket from his truck. She glanced into his eyes as he draped it over her shoulders.

"If you don't mind me asking, how did you come to live at Mrs. Barton's?"

"I don't mind at all. When I was thirteen, my world fell apart. It had been on the brink for years. The only living arrangements I ever had with my family involved dysfunction. Many times, alcohol was present. Sometimes accompanied by volatility, abuse, violence. I just couldn't continue to live in it anymore. I knew I needed a change to survive. So, my mother and I parted ways. Her last good gesture was making living arrangements for me with Miss Barton.

"As it turned out, she and my mom were old friends. She needed some help in the store, and I needed a place to stay while I finished school. Being near my church was a bonus. The two worked out the legality. Voila! God made a way!

"When Miss Barton saw me, she said it was like looking at a young Frances. She was thrilled to have me in her home. I was thrilled too."

Rachel could tell that was a lot for John to take in. In general, his life was what most people called normal. Hers had surely been the opposite.

"My turn. How are you holding up? I can't imagine how difficult life is for your family right now." John contemplated. "I feel helpless. Angry at times. Cancer grew in my dad's body untreated for months due to a misdiagnosis. I can take care of the crops and livestock and equipment 'til the cows come home. But I can't change what is happening to the most important man in my life." Rachel reached over and rested her hand on his.

John's gaze dropped. He was silent for a few moments. "Well, enough of that! Let's decide what you are going to be when you grow up!" Both chuckled.

The couple ate and talked and laughed until after midnight. When they arrived at Miss Barton's, the only light was from Rachel's porch to her private entrance. John opened the truck door, taking her hand. They walked up the path, adding as much time to the short journey as possible.

"Thank you for a lovely evening. It was nice. I had fun!"

John fidgeted. "I did too! I would love to take you out again. I'll pick you up this time, of course."

Rachel reached into her purse and pulled out a worn notecard and a pen. She wrote her phone number on the back and gave it to John. "I would love that." John leaned in, giving Rachel a gentle hug. "Good night." She returned the sentiment. He waited until she was inside and had locked the door.

John instantly missed Rachel's face. Her scent lingered in the doorway. He couldn't move. He knew everything had changed. Without hesitation, he knocked. "Rachel." She reopened the door. At first glance, they exchanged knowing smiles. "I don't want to seem pushy, but may I have a goodnight kiss?"

Rachel's heart melted at the sweetness and purity of this man, who already had her heart. She leaned in over the threshold. Their lips met in a delicate, warm moment. As they pulled away, their eyes locked, as well as their hearts.

There was a confidence in John's stroll as he returned to his truck. He carried a smile no one could remove. He knew this was the first night of many.

Chapter Seven

———— ≈ ————

John bounded into the kitchen. The family table that sat in the middle of the room was set with Mrs. Avery's usual five-star country breakfast. He grabbed a biscuit, sliced it through with a butter knife, and inserted a sausage. He never sat. He paused, staring for a moment, then released a reflective laugh.

Mrs. Avery and Kaye froze, exchanging a puzzling look. "Have a seat!" John darted around the kitchen like he was on a mission. He swept by his mother, kissing her on the cheek. "Got a lot to do today!"

Mr. Avery called from the den recliner—his new sleeping arrangement for his frail body, pain meds by his side. John stepped into the den, sitting down on the edge of the couch cushion. The biscuit was gone. Mr. Avery looked inquisitively at his son. A peaceful grin was there.

"How was your night?" John's smile widened, spreading to his whole face. He turned away. Mr. Avery laughed out loud. "That good, huh?"

By this time, Mrs. Avery and Kaye were standing at the doorway. The three shot surprising looks at one another. "Isn't God good!" Mr. Avery affirmed, addressing his son.

John had been out and about at first light. He visited the pasture to check on the cattle. A calf had been born in the night. It made a good stand and was feeding. At the hog barn, two sows were delivering. John stayed nearby until all the piglets were nursing. New life was emerging.

The September Saturday held a hint of fall. A crisp feeling. A slight chill. Almost undefinable, but still present. A new season. John breathed it in.

He made a quick list of items needed to service the truck that was used to pull peanut wagons. Most of the peanut acreage had been dug and inverted. Now the crop lay on top of the ground, drying in the sun. Hopefully, by midmorning, John and Luke would be picking again. With his list in hand, John headed for Barton Hardware.

A decade ago, the New Berry farm community convinced Miss Barton that stocking basic truck and tractor parts would be helpful for local farmers. Jimmy Browning had headed up the campaign. Miss Barton had been more than happy to comply.

Belts, hoses, filters, and the like kept the store as busy as their regular hardware inventory in the spring and fall. When John arrived, he immediately began to scan the store. His purpose this morning was twofold. Truck parts....and Rachel.

There she was. A ball cap covered her blonde hair. A ponytail dangled through the back. It swayed back and forth as she moved about helping her customers. Her jeans were holey on the knees. Not as a fashion statement, but from wear. A crisp Barton Hardware polo tucked in neatly was the final touch. John stopped and took it in. Rachel stood at the counter, writing a ticket for her customer. She then passed it to Miss Barton.

"How can I help you, sir?" Rachel grinned at the next customer. The gentleman was hesitant. He looked inquisitively behind the counter, as if looking for someone in particular. "Is there a man who could help me?"

The area was suddenly quiet. All eyes turned to the gentleman. "Uh, sure, sir!" Rachel smiled through her teeth. "Let me call Ed from the back. He will be with you in a moment." The man was satisfied.

Rachel greeted the next customer. "I need a fan belt and fuel filter for my truck." Rachel headed to the parts catalog. "What's your make and model?" When the customer responded, she began flipping through the pages. "Year?"

Rachel asked questions about the vehicle's engine until she identified the parts. She grabbed a long rod with a hook on the end and scooped the belt from a row at ceiling height. She moved to the addition where truck and tractor parts were housed to retrieve the filter. "Have a great day! Miss Barton will check you out."

Rachel made a house key for Widow Doster. Then she helped Pastor Jenkins choose the right stain for his office desk. All three customers were helped in a short twenty minutes.

With every customer interaction, every kind word, and every expression of her knowledge and initiative, John fell deeper in love. Yes, one day later, he was in love.

Rachel spotted John watching from a distance. Her face beamed. He turned away to look at the shelves of paint cans and began to fidget with the products. "Hi there!" John turned back with haste, nearly knocking over a display of sandpaper. Rachel caught it just in time. Both burst out in laughter.

"Is there a man who can help me?" John teased. Rachel playfully punched his upper arm. "Don't get me started!" He insisted on looking up his own parts, as he often did. "Are you interested in dinner tomorrow night after church?" The offer pleased Rachel. "Sure. I'll cook!" John wasn't expecting a home cooked meal, but he wouldn't refuse it.

As he was paying, Uncle Jimmy and Jackson came through the door. Jackson spotted Rachel and walked directly for her. Uncle Jimmy had business with John. As they discussed the critical timetable for gathering the crop, John's eyes glanced toward Rachel.

"You work in a hardware store? I would have never guessed. Most girls wouldn't even visit a store like this." Rachel took a stance. "Well, I'm not most girls!" She giggled. "It's a long story."

Jackson nodded in agreement. "Oh no, I assure you, I'm impressed! Hey, maybe we could grab a bi…." Rachel's focus broke as she saw John walking for the door. "See you tomorrow," she asserted. "Pot roast?" He stopped and looked directly into her eyes. "Sounds perfect!"

Rachel's attention returned to Jackson. "I'm so sorry. What were you saying? He fumbled with his words. "Maybe I'll see you at church tomorrow." Rachel nodded and smiled. "May-be!" She returned to her work, with John Avery constantly in her thoughts.

Rachel's roast had been cooking all Sunday afternoon in the crockpot. A peach cobbler was set to cool as she left for church.

There was much whispering as John settled in next to Rachel near the front row. Their friends were genuinely happy for them. During the song service, John's hand cupped Rachel's underneath the hymnal. She welcomed his touch.

Pastor Stephens shared from Romans 8:28. One of Rachel's favorite verses. She could see it unfolding before her eyes. John followed her home after service. Dinner's satisfying aroma greeted the two at the door.

Rachel had her own living area with a dinette. A bedroom. A bath. She and Miss Barton shared the kitchen that adjoined their separate living areas. Rachel rushed about laying out the cloth napkins and flatware. Sweetening the tea. Serving their plates.

John offered to help, but Rachel wouldn't have it. At least not this time.

John took Rachel's hand as he prayed a blessing over their meal. He ate everything on his plate and asked for seconds. Whether out of true hunger or an attempt to make a kind gesture, Rachel loved it. He was complimentary throughout the meal. That held a great deal of meaning. After all, his mother was one of the best cooks in the county.

John helped clear the table. The two stood side by side at the sink. Washing. Rinsing. Overlapping hands. Laughing. Splashing suds on each other. Miss Barton slid her pocket door open. "Hey there! You two seem to be enjoying your evening." She gave Rachel a wink. Rachel and John shared a mischievous glance, like two kids who had been called to the principal's office.

"I'm going to grab a bite from the frig, if you don't mind. Rachel reached over and opened the oven door. "I made a plate of roast, potatoes, and carrots with a few slices of fresh bread for the gravy. Cobbler is for dessert." Miss Barton was humbled. "Rachel, you are too good to me! I do appreciate you!"

Miss Barton retrieved the meal and disappeared. "I love that woman! Her hospitality amazes me. Most times, she acts like she is MY guest instead of the other way around. God was certainly working when He made this connection."

"Are you up for a picnic? By moonlight? I'd like to take you out to the pasture to see the new calf. We could eat our dessert there." Rachel was giddy. *A picnic. Moonlight. Baby calf.*

Could it get any better? "Absolutely! I'll pack a basket."

Moonlight illuminated the field. The light-colored hide of the cattle was visible as the lunar glow fell. John dropped the tailgate. He pulled a lantern and a horse blanket from the truck cab. Dessert was especially sweet.

John was not as shy as most thought. As she had thought. Then again, maybe he was just at ease with Rachel. Being in each other's presence was as easy as breathing. No effort.

The two listened as the cattle lowed. John paused, listening with intent. "I think one of the heifers might be in trouble." John took the flashlight and walked toward the edge of the pines. He yelled back. "She's trying to deliver! This is her first!"

"Rachel, can you drive the truck over here? I need the headlights! She's going to need my help!" Rachel jumped from the tailgate and climbed in the cab. She got the truck turned around and in position near the trees. The cow's breathing was labored. John was on the ground, rubbing her. "Come on, girl! You can do this!

"Rachel, come kneel at her head. Rub along her neck and body in long strokes. Talk to her. We need to keep her calm." Rachel did as instructed. All the while watching every move John made. Rachel's eyes widened as John lay down on his back. He inserted his hand in the birth canal and began to move inward toward the calf. "She's contracting, but no progress." He didn't stop until his entire arm, to his shoulder, was inside the mother.

"The calf isn't moving." John paused. "It's dead!" Rachel instantly laid her head on the mother's neck. Rubbing. Crying. Consoling. "I'm going to help her deliver. You're doing a great job, Rachel!"

Through her tears, she watched the process as John slowly pulled the calf from its mother. The lifeless body lay in the grass. The mother moaned. Rachel cried. John inserted his arm again. "There's another one! Twins! He's a twin!"

John worked inside the mother, ensuring the calf was positioned correctly for birth. She moaned and pushed as her body contracted. The calf slipped out and into John's arms. Its head turned and its legs kicked. This time, Rachel cried happy tears.

John pulled up to Rachel's house. "Don't get out. I know you are ready to get home and get cleaned up." John jumped out to open her door before she could offer another protest. "I kept you out late again." He glanced apologetically. "Maybe we will have a normal date next time."

"Oh no, I wouldn't trade this night for the world." He cast a questioning look Rachel's way. "Friday night?" She nodded.

"I have a volunteer coming this week to help pick peanuts. Jackson Stone. Uncle Jimmy introduced us. He came by today to look things over.

He will be in town for another week and has offered to help me. That's what Uncle Jimmy and I were talking about yesterday at the hardware store. He's a good guy."

The forecast showed rain coming in at the end of the week. There was already too much moisture. In the ground. In the peanuts. If the peanuts were not picked, they could be lost to mold. Or they could pull off the vine and be left in the field. Either way, losing peanuts was not the best scenario for the business.

"Jackson and I hit it off from the start. It's like we have known each other for years. I would imagine if I had a brother."

The week was busy. John and Jackson stayed in the field. Lunches, as usual, were prepared by Mrs. Avery. Despite dust, dirt, and grime, Mrs. Avery brought the young men right to the kitchen table. She wouldn't let anyone go hungry.

Mr. Avery found joy in listening to his son carry on with his new friend. "Got a woman in your life, Jackson?" He inquired from the recliner. Jackson looked over at John with a sarcastic smile. "No, sir! The good ones are already taken!" John grinned. "You got that right!"

The beginning of Rachel's week was full of bookstore hours and classes. John called each evening from the phone booth. With the only family phone situated in the kitchen, there was no privacy at the Avery's. He and Rachel couldn't get enough of each other.

"Rachel, Jackson will be heading back to Gainesville on Saturday. I thought the three of us might go out to dinner on Friday. I want to show my appreciation for the help he has given our family. And I want you two to get to know each other better."

"Sounds like a great plan."

"If you aren't busy on Friday morning, come by the farm. I thought you might want to learn to drive the tractor. You could even pick a few peanuts." Rachel was all in.

John pulled into Rachel's driveway at six o'clock sharp, then headed to Uncle Jimmy's for Jackson. The three squeezed into the cab of the F150 and headed to Morton's Family Steakhouse. Ending peanut picking season was a good reason for a Certified Angus steak. The three agreed on that.

The food was delicious, and the conversation even better. There was laughter and joking. They talked about construction, world missions, and everything in between. They reminisced about Rachel dumping the last basket of peanuts from the picker into the wagon. Peanuts she picked herself. Her maiden farm voyage.

They almost had the world's problems solved when the restaurant owner stepped up to the table. "John, there's a call for you. Sounds urgent!" He rushed to the phone. "John, we are headed back to the hospital with your dad. Lots of pain and bleeding." The color drained from John's face. His mother's words were unexpected. He turned and was face-to-face with Jackson and Rachel. "John, whatever you need to do, we're with you."

The friends piled back in the truck and sped to Health Center South. They were waiting at the emergency room entrance when the Averys pulled in. John and Jackson lifted Mr. Avery from the car into a wheelchair. The nurse took him to the back immediately, with Mrs. Avery following alongside them.

One o'clock came quickly. The waiting room was now quiet. John offered to let Jackson and Rachel take his truck home. He never would have imagined what the night would hold. Both refused. Providence had orchestrated their presence. They were fine with that.

By sunrise, pain was managed with higher doses of morphine. Ultrasound revealed the spreading of the bowel malignancy. All previous efforts had not deterred the cancer. The oncologist released Mr. Avery to rest at home.

The family was tired. Emotionally numb and in disbelief. Their prayers were for healing here and now. For their husband, father, and friend to live to farm again. To see his children married. To grow old. Now, other preparations were imminent.

Sunday morning arrived. Everyone had gotten a good night's sleep. Jackson had returned to Georgia for Monday morning classes. Rachel was in church, praying for the family she had come to love.

"John, your dad wants to talk to you." Mrs. Avery sat on the couch. She seemed to still be in shock. Going through the motions. Afraid that if she let herself process it all too thoroughly, she would fall apart.

John quietly entered the bedroom, which now held a hospital bed. Mr. Avery was still, with his eyes closed. John stared at this man, who no longer resembled his father. *God, where are you?*

Mr. Avery opened his eyes. "Son." John stepped closer and took his father's hand.

"We have some preparations to make." John's face grimaced. He shook his head. "Not for my death, son. For your life. God answered my prayers. You love her, don't you? You love Rachel." John couldn't deny his feelings. It happened fast, but it was real.

Within two weeks, John and his father had secured a few acres that adjoined Avery Farms. A perfect homeplace. It sat beautifully in the middle of everything the men built together.

"Now, go find a car so you can court Rachel appropriately."

The couple enjoyed a late lunch at Rachel's after Sunday morning service. "You ok, John? You seem a little quiet this afternoon." John evaded the question as the two loaded up for an afternoon drive. The simple beauty of God's creation and each other's company were the perfect dessert. John pulled into the church parking lot and turned off the engine.

"Rachel, two months ago, my life changed forever." He looked toward the church. "It happened the day you walked to the back to greet me. It had been the worst weekend of my life. Then you extended your hand. I knew right then and there I wanted you. For life."

John reached into his pocket and pulled out an old notecard. Rachel's phone number. He flipped the card over. Handwritten on the worn paper was Romans 8:28. Rachel took a deep breath. She knew the card. John read aloud as tears pooled in Rachel's eyes.

"And we know that in all things

God works for the good of those who love him,

who have been called according to his purpose."

John removed a small jewelry box from the console and opened it toward Rachel. A solitaire diamond ring was waiting. "Rachel? Will you be my wife?"

When the two arrived at John's house to share the news, Mr. Avery was being loaded into an ambulance. John grabbed his father's hand. "Help me sit up, son. Let me see this land I have loved one last time." His eyes slowly scanned from east to west. His gaze lingered as the sun dropped below the horizon.

"John, take care of your mama." John nodded his head as tears fell on their clasped hands. "Rachel." He smiled as he glanced at her ring finger. "Take care of my boy." Rachel couldn't speak but nodded as warm tears covered her face.

Mrs. Avery and Kaye wept at the finality as they joined the family patriarch and departed. John and Rachel raced behind, caravanning toward the hospital.

Without warning, the ambulance lights went dark.

The siren became silent.

He was gone.

Chapter Eight

———— ≈ ————

T *ake care of your mother.* Mr. Avery's final words played over and over in John's head.

He tried each day to take on the role of a businessman. To fill his father's shoes. To protect his mother's future. As the sun set on the acres each evening, he was just a farmer's son who missed his dad.

John worried about his mother. She kept her pain hidden. She went through the motions of her days with precision. As if her tasks were the friends who kept her sane. Keep moving and cooking and washing.

It was at night, when the lights went out on the chores, that Mrs. Avery's quiet whimpers sifted through the silence. Kaye retired to her room each evening. Avoiding the reality of their circumstance by escaping into her world of fiction. Each dealt with the void in the way their survival dictated.

John's salvation from the grief? Rachel. John recognized that God had done a miracle in his life. At his lowest point, God sent a woman to rescue him.

John made sure to schedule his hardware store visits to coincide with Rachel's work schedule. They spoke on the phone nightly. Rachel visited the Avery's at least one night a week and had Sunday lunch with the family. John picked her up and returned her home appropriately. Weekly services, of course, would find John Avery and Rachel Sanders on the second row of First Community Church.

John would have loved for his father to be by his side as he made his vow to Rachel in the coming nuptials. He recalled how his father had taken the reins over the last month of his life. He knew he wouldn't be there to stand with his son. He had done the next best thing. He had helped lay the foundation for John and Rachel's future. A good father.

Mr. Avery was the reason John understood the nature of God the Father. He stood guard over his family in prayer. He loved. Provided. Protected. And walked as an example worthy of following. John never questioned His love or his intent.

Rachel's framework for a father was not built on the same foundation. John didn't know all the details of her life…yet. He knew that she had walked a different path. One foreign to him. John knew he loved Rachel here and now and was ready to build a safe place on a strong foundation.

John was headed out to the field after lunch when his mother yelled from the back door. "It's Rachel! She sounds frantic!" John ran back to the kitchen, grabbing the phone. "John, please come! It's Miss Barton! Hurry!"

Panic erupted in John's eyes. "What is it, son?" His heart pounded. "I don't know. Miss Barton? Rachel needs me!" John rushed to his truck and peeled out of the driveway with one thought. *Rachel!* The five miles seemed like fifty. The speedometer never occurred to him.

The county rescue squad was in the driveway when John pulled in. Uncle Jimmy pulled in right behind him, barely stopping before he jumped from his pickup. "I heard the call go out on the scanner!" He ran into the house on John's heels.

Rachel was frozen when John's eyes landed on her, her gaze hollow. A quiver began at her chin, moving to her high cheek bones as she saw him rushing toward her. Dropping to his knees, John pulled her tight in his arms. She felt the gentle strength in his hand as he encouraged her to rest her head on his shoulder. As they leaned into one another, Rachel's sobs erupted.

Uncle Jimmy moved past the couple as if seeing no one. He entered the living room just as a cloth was lifted over Miss Barton's face. His eyes widened at the sight. He took a deep breath and closed his eyes, trying to hold the emotions in place. He retreated a few steps and reached behind, taking hold of a ladderback chair. He never took his eyes off the lifeless form as he found the seat with his hand and lowered himself to it.

The town's youngest paramedic, Tucker Anderson, paused from his work and made eye contact. "Looks like a heart attack. She was in her armchair with a full cup of coffee on the side table. Here one minute…gone the next. Rachel found her when she came in from her morning classes."

Jimmy barely nodded. His sight held steady. Tucker worked methodically and respectfully. Young and old held Miss Barton in high regard.

When Jimmy could stand, he returned to the room where Rachel and John were processing the event. He slumped next to Rachel at the table, laying his head on his crossed arms.

"I'm sorry. I know you and Miss Barton had a special relationship." Jimmy raised his head and gave a solemn response. "Yes, she was a good friend."

John and Rachel exchanged a questioning glance. "Friends?" We thought you and Miss Barton were more than friends. For years." Jimmy shook his head. "No. That wasn't it at all." He got a faraway look in his eyes. He inhaled as if this were his last breath, then pushed out the air along with the emotion.

There was a gentle knock at the door. An older, bearded man leaned around the frame as if seeking permission to enter. Mr. Donnell had been the county coroner for more years than anyone could count. He was usually on the scene in haste to tend to the business at hand. However, it was his compassion and care for the bereaved that kept him in office. He approached the table, resting his hand firmly on the shoulder of the hunched figure. "I'm sorry, Jimmy. I'm so sorry." He looked up, nodding in acceptance, but didn't speak.

As word spread, a steady trail of neighbors converged on the home. Food began to black out the counter space. People were scattered like ants. No seeming rhyme or reason to the movement, the chatter, or sometimes even the laughter. It was simply the way of the South. It was what was done. Whether chosen or not.

Mrs. Avery and Kaye had been present all afternoon, tending to every need and working steadily with no direction needed. They, along with other staples of the community, organized the kitchen. Food was arranged. And rearranged. Finally, the impossible task of storing leftovers was attempted by those who were not faint of heart.

Sunset brought a thinning crowd. John walked alongside Uncle Jimmy to his truck. "Make sure Rachel gets some rest. I'm going to come by early." He stopped short of the door and extended his hand to John. "Thanks for taking care of our girl. Rachel has a special place in my heart." John nodded with a convincing, respectful smile. "I completely understand."

"Seven o'clock. I'd like for you to be here too." Jimmy's voice trembled. "Rachel and I have some talking to do."

Rachel felt as though she had just rested her head on the pillow when the filtering sun broke through the curtain and appeared on her comforter. A few moments passed before her mind remembered why there was a knot in her stomach.

Rachel took in the smell of fresh coffee and biscuits. *Mrs. Avery.* She wouldn't allow her soon-to-be daughter-in-law to be alone after such an emotional shock. She slept on the couch, then headed home early after she prepared the morning nourishment.

Jimmy had been at the table for half an hour when Rachel emerged. Biscuit crumbs and a empty coffee mug were before him. John entered from the kitchen with a hot cup just the way Rachel liked it. More cream than coffee.

She moved into John's open arms and nuzzled the side of her face against the breast of his jacket. They lingered for a few moments in a peaceful embrace. He kissed her on the head, then settled her at the table, sitting close to his bride-to-be.

The three were alone. Before Rachel had taken a sip, Jimmy's story began to spill out. "Barton and I were friends. Good friends. I can see that you might have thought there was more since I was next door for dinner once a week. There wasn't.

"My older brother and I had a falling out back in the sixties. We never could get past it. I left home and moved here. I met my late wife, Mary." Jimmy stared out of the window as if he had stepped back in time. A soothing grin enveloped his face. He closed his eyes, breathing in the memory.

"She was stunning. I fell deep from the first moment I saw her at her father's store. Everyone thought she needed a younger man. I was ten years her senior. But she fell as hard as I did. I didn't understand how she could, but I thanked God every day. She was the best thing that ever happened to me.

"Mary's father was skeptical. I guess he thought I wasn't good enough for his baby girl." Jimmy held back tears. "I'm sure I wasn't. I poured asphalt for driveways and county road repair with Thomas Stein." Rachel smiled. "It was dirty, hot work. I needed to raise enough money for a down payment on a small farm outside of town. He did what he could to help me. I wanted everything to be in place when I asked for Mary's hand.

"Her sister, Martha, saw how much Mary loved me. How happy we were together. It was because of her that their father eventually accepted me. Martha. Martha Barton."

Rachel and John froze. *Martha Barton? Miss Barton was Jimmy's sister-in-law?* They were speechless. "We married after I finalized the sale of the farm. There was an old tenant house on the property. Together, we fixed it up and made it our home. What a time we had! Some of the old-timers remember. Pretty much, not many folks know the details."

Jimmy looked at Rachel. "My brother's youngest and her mother came to visit during those first few years we were married. They were the only connection I had to my past. Mary found a dear friend during that time. Mary, Fran, and Martha were like peas in a pod.

"We had been married two years when Mary told me she was pregnant." Jimmy's expression dimmed. His eyes narrowed as sadness fell. "The pregnancy took her strength. I made sure she rested as much as possible. I headed to the field on that March afternoon. She was six months in. I returned right at dark.

"Normally, when Mary heard the tractor coming around the barn, she opened the door, stepping onto the porch." He started to speak, then stopped. His hands began to tremble. He lowered his head as if trying to remember but needing to forget.

"The door didn't open. The house was dark." He lowered his gaze, shaking his head. "I knew something was terribly wrong."

"Uncle Jimmy! You don't have to go on. We can see how hard this is for you. You don't have to talk about this now." Rachel took his hands in hers. Jimmy raised his head with determination. "No! There are some things that need to be said. It's past time!

"I found her. The doctor said our baby had likely died a week earlier. Infection would have spread through Mary's body. Sepsis they called it. She began to hemorrhage after I left the house. We had no phone. She couldn't call for help. She bled to death.

"In my eyes, my life ended that day. I never knew sorrow could go so deep. As high as we went in love, grief took me just as low. Her father grieved himself to death.

"Martha took over Barton Hardware. All she knew was that she had to work to survive it. I couldn't work at all. I couldn't muster the strength or desire to plant a single seed that year. I didn't want any evidence of life. I needed to stay right there. In that moment. In that place. Where she left my world."

Jimmy's tone changed, and a confidence came over him. "Rachel, there is no need to worry about where you will stay now that Martha's gone." She turned with intrigue.

"You see, Rachel...I own this house." The words made no sense to her. "You? I don't understand. Why didn't you tell me?"

"I bought the house from Martha when you moved here. I wanted to ensure that if anything were to happen to me, my niece would be taken care of." Rachel couldn't understand what he was saying.

"Rachel, my brother was Buster. Your daddy. I'm your uncle."

John leaned in, putting an arm around Rachel and pulling her close. She looked toward him, hoping he could help her understand. Before she could even blink, tears began to fill her eyes.

"What? Why are you saying that? That can't be true! I was told my daddy only had one brother. His name was Frank!" Jimmy lowered his head. "Yes. Frank James Browning...Jimmy.

"You and your mother visited often. Frances, or Fran, as we called her, was the best friend my Mary ever had. We couldn't have loved you anymore if you had been our own. You were the first in New Berry to ever call me Uncle Jimmy. It stuck!

"Buster and I fell out because of the way he treated Frances. He returned home after the long affair. It was the right thing. But he had convinced her they would be together. Forever. She believed him. Maybe he even believed it. When he broke off the relationship, she was eight months pregnant with you. It almost killed her."

The pain in Pine County for Frances was unbearable. Only a handful of people knew about her. When the affair was over, it was like she hadn't existed in Buster's life. Until Rachel's birth. She was the undeniable evidence, though her father never acknowledged her publicly.

Jimmy and Mary had hoped Frances would make her home near them. Then the tragedy. When Mary died, all three could have gone in the casket with her. A part of each one died. Martha worked. Jimmy retreated. Frances ran. Their little world had fallen apart.

No one blamed Frances for moving away to Florida with Pate and Rachel. Her life had been hard from the beginning. When she was a teenager, her father left the family. His wife and children. Her father's rejection was long-lasting. Buster's rejection compounded her trauma.

"When Frances returned to New Berry. To you. It was evident the pain was just as real as a decade before. The wound had never healed. On an unexpected afternoon, Buster and Frances crossed paths. Though the dangerous flame between them still burned, she refused to submit to it. Again, she ran. The distance that wounded you, saved her.

"If Frances had ever trusted anyone, it was Martha and me. She wanted you to know us. Frances wanted you with her, but she knew you were right where you needed to be. A safe home. A good school. Your church. And me watching over you. It kept you away from the dysfunction she wasn't equipped to address. For Martha and me, it felt as though God were giving us a reprieve by taking us back to the best time of our lives. God worked a bad situation for your good."

Jimmy reached into his jacket pocket and pulled out a black-and-white photo. It was tattered. Worn. A young man held a small child in his arms. Her blonde curls were waving. Both in the midst of uncontrollable laughter. Three beautiful women stood arm in arm. One holding her hand proudly under her abdomen, accentuating her expectancy. Jimmy's voice quivered. "This was the happiest day of my life." For a long while, his eyes remained steady.

Jimmy took Rachel's hands in his. He looked directly into her eyes. "I went to visit Buster a few days before his death. We made things right. He was sorry for what happened with your mother…and you. I had the privilege of leading him in the Sinner's Prayer. We will all see each other again. I'm sorry I kept my identity from you, Rachel. I thought it was best."

Rachel turned to John. He held her as sobs came flooding out. Sadness and joy in concert overwhelmed her.

"Rachel, God was working all things together for your good before you ever knew His name. He loved you from the start. From the time of your troubled beginnings, He was making a way for you. He's a good, good Father!"

He reached into his pocket and retrieved a shiny gold key. "The deed will be ready tomorrow." He placed the key in the palm of her hand and closed her fingers around it.

Leaning in, he delivered a gracious kiss to her forehead. "Welcome home, Rachel."

Chapter Nine

———— ≈ ————

Jackson shifted his luggage in the back of the jeep. One oversized backpack to carry on. One large duffle bag to check. Small construction tools were tucked in around T-shirts and socks. Each brand-new tool would only make a one-way trip.

John's gear was added. Mirroring Jackson's. Weight limits for the flight were not the only consideration. With two flights and primitive river travel, the need to minimize was facilitated.

John pulled a small leather booklet from his jacket pocket a second time and began flipping through paperwork. *Passport. Airline Ticket. Immunization Documentation.* "Don't fret! It's all there!"

John lowered his sunglasses to the tip of his nose. Peeking over the metal frames, he directed a stern look toward Jackson. "You've done this before. I'm a rookie! Rachel will never forgive me if I mess this up and don't get back to the States for the wedding." Jackson shook his head. "Yeah, yeah! Don't worry about it. If you don't make it back, I'll stand in for you!" He gave an exaggerated wink.

John raised one eyebrow and made eye contact. "Ha! In your dreams, Georgia Boy! The two jumped in the seats of the ragtop and headed toward Rachel's house, which just months earlier she shared with Miss Barton.

Precision was the name of this game. Jackson's college graduation and John's planting season were completed in early May. With the wedding four weeks out, the guys were heading out on a short mission trip to a remote village in the jungles of Peru.

Jackson and John's trip was fully funded by Jimmy Browning. He took great joy in sending young adults from New Berry to the mission field. He believed work outside the walls of the church, including foreign missions, was part of the call of the church. "The chores are at the house. The work is in the field," he recited.

Jimmy first met Jackson's parents, Lane and Patsy Stone, and their feisty seven-year-old, Jackson, fifteen years earlier when he attended his first trip to South America. It was a few years after Mary died. He didn't want to go. He didn't want to experience life without her. He simply knew that if he didn't get up from the grief, he would die too.

Jimmy was assured that God wasn't finished with him. The work he did on that trip. The relationships he formed that week. The love he experienced for and from the indigenous people began to push the pain out of the forefront of his heart.

Though John was very private about his grief, Jimmy prayed the same miracle for him after the loss of his father, John Sr. Jimmy learned through experience that giving out of his own need created an atmosphere for God's healing to sprout. He couldn't wait to see what God did in John's life.

The guys found Uncle Jimmy and Rachel at the kitchen table packing a suitcase of coloring books, spiral notebooks, and crayons. As the village teacher had requested. A second suitcase was loaded with seventy sets of reading glasses, toothbrushes, and toothpaste that had been donated by their church.

Rachel rose from the table and greeted John with a kiss and an embrace that looked exactly like a woman just weeks away from her wedding. John looked at the suitcases of essentials, shaking his head in disbelief. "The simplest needs we take for granted here in the States."

"I have your flight information and itinerary on the refrigerator. Call if you can. I'll be busy finishing up wedding details. We'll see you two in ten days. Behave!" She dropped her head and shot Jackson an accusing look. "What?" His defense was mixed with an air of mischief and a sarcastic smile. "Just get him back to me safe and sound. Wedding, remember? John, groom. Jackson, best man. Say that over and over to yourself."

She approached Jackson's tall frame, clutching his cheeks in the palms of her hands. She pulled his head low and landed a kiss on his forehead. "Have fun. Love you both!" Jackson nodded. "Yes, ma'am!"

Jimmy gathered Rachel, John, and Jackson in a huddle. "Lord, we thank you that you are faithful and that you are always working for our good. We ask that you go before Jackson and John. Protect them from any harm. Guide their steps. Make their work for your kingdom productive. Let the people be drawn to you through your love seen in them. Bring them home safely. Amen."

"I love our sweet community, but there is a big world out there with people who need our resources and talents. Most of all, they need the love of Jesus. Get ready, John. This trip is going to change. Your. Life!"

As the plane circled for landing, Jackson watched with amusement as John looked out over the city. Lima was a sight to behold. Nestled along the Pacific Coast, its tip hung just below the equator. The Andes Mountains provided a stunning backdrop. John's eyes were as wide open as his heart.

"You can let go of the seat arm now. Your knuckles are white." Jackson couldn't pass up a chance to tease his friend. And he hoped his banter would put John at ease. Nearly seven hours in the air had provided for much conversation. They never ran out of words.

John was relieved when the plane touched down. More so when they had retrieved the luggage and were headed out. "It really wasn't as bad as I thought." The automatic doors retreated. A new world greeted them.

The streets were abuzz with wall-to-wall taxis and buses, their agitated drivers expressing urgency with horns reverberating from every direction. Rickshaw drivers motored their vehicles in and out of traffic. Bikes were abundant. Sidewalks were flooded with faces breathing in the thick smog.

The moderate temperatures at the beginning of the dry season were familiar. Though it was May, the opposing season of the Southern Hemisphere was true to an Alabama autumn. No watch resets were necessary in a matching time zone.

Jackson and John caught a taxi and headed toward the east. The two would assemble at the Amara Hotel with other men who hailed from across the Northern Hemisphere. Men from every walk of life who would comprise a six-day work team. The guys had hoped the traffic would be mild for their three-mile drive. Lima traffic was never mild.

Jackson was *old hat* at mission work. He cut his teeth along with the indigenous children of the Amazon tributaries. The villages along Pastor Carlos Estrada's circuit were family to Jackson. Each trip was like coming home.

Resources from Stone Construction of Gainesville, his parents' company, were used to fund quarterly mission trips focused on the needs of the Peruvian people. Lane and Patsy Stone were not wealthy by any standards. But they were givers. Their faith compelled them to give. And give generously. Their ever-thriving business was evidence that they could not outgive God.

Jackson had invited friends to accompany him on trips in the past. Facilitating the experience for John was different. He couldn't be happier to witness John's maiden voyage. God had intersected their paths. For a purpose greater than either could fathom.

Jackson spoke with the driver in fluent Spanish as the luggage was unloaded. John was thankful he didn't have to navigate language barriers. He was highly impressed with Jackson's use of the language and the kind manner in which he interacted with the people. Regardless of their station.

The two entered a small conference room off the main lobby of the old hotel. Jackson and John were the last to arrive. The room erupted. Jackson knew every face. Greetings and hugs followed. Jackson proudly introduced John. Each man embraced him, welcomed him, and thanked him for giving his time. This wasn't like a family reunion. It WAS a family reunion. The blood of Christ made them Christians. The love of Christ made them brothers.

Lawrence, the trip leader for Missions Alive, prepped the team. He had led many into the jungle. His planning and organizational skills were unmatched. But it was his love for the indigenous people and the relationships he had formed over decades that made all the difference. Anticipation made achieving sleep difficult. The men couldn't wait for sunrise.

After breakfast, the team was led in devotion and prayer. Excitement grew as they set out.

Iquitos, one of the largest cities in Peru, could only be reached by water or air. From the coastal city of Lima over the Andes Mountains, a short one-and-a-half-hour flight positioned the group for the next leg of the trip. A dozen workers found themselves in the heart of the rainforest at the Amazon River. Pastor Carlos could not have been prouder. He welcomed his friends with a grateful heart and tear-filled eyes.

Pastor Carlos and his son, Amelio, made the trip upriver to Iquitos the prior day. Building project materials were purchased with funds forwarded from Missions Alive and loaded onto a longboat. When night fell, they alternated sleeping, leaving one man awake to guard the much-coveted wares. Two dozen chickens were purchased hours before the team's arrival. For this, the widows would be grateful.

A quick bite of lunch was eaten. Final phone calls made. Luggage was loaded onto a second longboat for the travelers. The narrow structures greater than fifty feet were mechanized by an extended shaft propeller assembled into what looked like a lawnmower motor. It provided a slow, steady movement. Prayers were offered over the vessel, as was appropriate and necessary.

The rainy season had just ended. The river was still eight to nine feet higher on its banks. Nearly forty inches of rain had fallen in the previous quarter. Miles of lowlands were invaded by Amazon waters. Fertile nutrients that would be deposited in the basin as the waters receded would produce abundant crops for its inhabitants…and the world.

Jackson sat near his friend to observe his experience. John was overwhelmed. The man who chose to keep his deepest emotions private was struggling to hold back tears. God was moving in his heart in a way that was new. So much love he could scarcely contain it.

And the beauty of God's creation…it was breathtaking. John closed his eyes, taking in the myriad of sounds emerging from the jungle: the water lapping on the sides of the boat, the consistent *click, click, click* of the boat motor, and the low cluck of the caged fowl.

And the verses sung by Pastor Carlos in his second language. One by one, each man joined the singing, almost in a whisper.

Amazing grace, how sweet the sound

That saved a wretch like me.

I once was lost, but now I'm found.

Was blind but now I see.

The team was two hours into the journey. The midmorning sun was pressing in. The river was busy. The Highway of the Amazon Rainforest. Longboats loaded with papaya, passion fruit, oranges, and cacao made their way upstream to the port city.

Vessels stacked solely with green bananas towering six feet over the boat rim were common. Each stalk easily revealed hundreds of fruits. Seeing this harvest at its origin was enlightening. The farmer in John was mesmerized.

"I wish Rachel were here to see this." Jackson nodded in agreement. "But!" The tranquility of the setting was broken as the two declared in unison. "She's afraid of heights!" They snickered, thinking of Rachel's protests against flying and how she maintained a strong argument.

By early afternoon, Pastor Carlos was tying the boats off on a mahogany stump that had been cut a generation ago. The current carried the longboats until they paralleled the bank. Lush, low growth provided a buffer under the canopy of palms and rubber trees.

The path from the mud landing was a twenty-five-yard trek at a strong 45-degree incline. The recent rains and previous traffic created an obstacle that would test each man's determination and stamina. The village was still another mile beyond the upper bank.

No time was wasted. Pastor Carlos directed the movement of the cargo. An assembly line method was utilized, passing items from person to person to the top of the bank. Men from the village arrived and joined the pursuit. As each stood in the assigned place, their lower extremities began to disappear in the soft mud. *Quagmire.* Staying in a singular position until the unloading was complete was the only option.

Villagers worked at the top of the embankment, stacking and loading mules and one rickety single-axle, two-wheeled wagon. Finally, a rope was lowered. A burden bearer pulled and brayed, lifting each man from his thick mud enclosure.

As the second day closed, the village came into sight. Jackson put his muddy arm around John's equally mud-clad shoulder. A few chicken feathers that had departed from their protesting captives clung to their bodies. They were a sight.

John's breath caught as he looked out over the landscape. The grasses were thick and lush. Vibrant. Palm, banana, and papaya trees created a sea of green, with thatched-roof huts sprinkled throughout.

Beyond the plateau of the village, the land dropped off in a gentle slope, moving into a valley whose foundation was concealed by the upper story tree canopy. The sounds of the clean waters of the ever-moving mountain river were a song of life for the villagers.

Mountains in the distance exploded with the production of chlorophyll in every shade of green. Beyond, they emerged to greater heights, with white peaks capping their majesty against a vast blue canvas. It was deep. And wide. And low. And high. Everything in one painting of God's creation, but no words to ascribe. John was sure he was witnessing the foothills of the new home in which his daddy resided.

In the center of the village stood a structure. Larger than the huts. Openings were spaced along the outer walls, where windows would be. A hand painted sign adorned the dwelling.

"*Jesus es el Senor!*" *Jesus is Lord!* The church.

"It's paradise. Most of these people live in a dwelling smaller than what we would use to store our garden tools. But they have more joy than most who live in what we would consider a mansion. THIS is God's country!" Jackson felt his speech in every fiber of his being. John could only utter one word, "Jesus."

The villagers moved about in the distance. Men completed chores and gathered chairs for the service. Women prepared the evening meal. Children played their favorite game of soccer. When Pastor Carlos and their visitors were spotted, all the commotion stopped. Every villager rushed to offer greetings.

Tents for the workers were established at the edge of the village clearing. Much-needed river baths provided refreshment. Removing the evidence of the day's work was a struggle.

The icy, rushing waters did the job.

Dinner was unusual but delicious. All the villagers gathered to share the meal and honor their guests. Fresh exotic fruits, known and unknown to the visitors, garnished the table. Bananas were abundant. A hardy piranha stew thickened with manioc root was comfort food for all.

The villagers were honored by the presence of the foreigners, who traveled a great distance. For them. The gifts of services offered were welcomed. Appreciated. But gifts were not the only need.

The very presence of the men gave them a sense of validation. Validation that they—a people, a village, a part of the Body of Christ hidden far away in a sea of green—were of value. Of importance. They were worth knowing.

The whole village gathered in the church, which was the schoolhouse by day. As the music began and the worshippers engaged, the room exploded with high-intensity praise.

Unadulterated. Unhindered.

Pastor Carlos stood ready to translate as Pastor Lawrence shared with the people. "Quagmire! A boggy area of land that gives way under our feet. A place where we sink. Where we get stuck. A difficult place to get free." Lawrence spoke slowly and decisively while Pastor Carlos translated each word.

"Today, we encountered the quagmire. As we exited the longboat, our legs were taken in by the soft mud until we could no longer move. The ground gave way beneath us. We were stuck. We couldn't get free. Not on our own.

"God is here to lift you. To lift us. From the mud. From the mire. From that which has us stuck." His voice increased in power and assurance. As the translations rang out, the villagers rose to their feet. Shouts came from the people. Praises ignited. The greater the response of the people, the more God's Spirit worked among them.

"Is it sin? Is it fear? Is it pain or sickness? Is it the unknown? No matter your quagmire, Jesus is here to lift you out. To set you free. To do what you cannot do for yourself. To do what you have tried to do but failed.

"Come now to the one who died to deliver you from your quagmire! Come now to Jesus!"

In five minutes, the Word of God went forth. In five minutes, the people responded to the Spirit. In five minutes, the entire village was on its face before God. Crying out. Surrendering to Jesus.

The service continued for two more hours. Jackson and John praised, worshipped, and prayed alongside their village family. They experienced freedom. Complete surrender.

The village submitted to the darkness. Life paused on the plateau. Sounds were evidence of the awakening nightlife of the Amazon Forest. The birds of the upper canopy told their stories. The distant cry of the mountain lion proclaimed his dominance. Braying mules and whining dogs submitted to the unseen predator.

Roosters marked the end of the day as all settled into quietness. Under the open sky and a billion stars, the cries of the wild lulled tired workers. Sleep overtook their bodies. Peace settled in their souls as the embers of the cooking fires smoldered. "Good night, Jackson." He peaked from his near slumber, "Good night, John Boy."

The next few days in the village were much like the first. Overflowing with love. Encouragement. Fellowship. Pastor Carlos shared the needs of the people to be addressed. Tasks seemed easier than normal when working alongside village counterparts.

Wooden benches in the church were the first order of business. Chairs carried from family huts to church services were the norm. Schoolchildren sat on the floor. The men were humbled by the appreciation shown by the villagers.

The construction of chicken enclosures was the second task for the team. Each widow received four chickens, an enclosure, a bag of feed, and access to a shared incubator. The widows looked on, tears flowing. The guarantee of food and the eventual generation of income was a dream. Self-sufficiency was always the mission.

Each day repeated. Sleep. Eat. Work. Then revival services.

When the day of departure arrived, the projects were complete. Roofs repaired. Fall crops planted. John wrapped his arms around each villager. In a few short days, he had become acquainted with their faces, their expressions, and their love for the Savior. Their imprint was now on his life.

He came to give, but had received much more. He found a piece of heaven. A place that could only be better if his Rachel were by his side.

Sulay, an older gentleman, gravitated toward John over the week. They had worked side by side and shared a place at the dinner table each night. Sulay enlisted Pastor Carlos to translate his goodbye message to John. "I thank my God for sending you. You have warmed a place in my heart that was cold. A place I thought was dead. I lost my son last year to the Great River. Working beside you made me feel my son's love once more. Thank you. You have helped my heart begin to heal."

They embraced. They wept. Sulay remembered his son. John remembered his father. Heaven rejoiced.

On the long boat ride back to Iquitos, John inquired about the response of the people. Of their pliable hearts. Of their complete surrender. A purity rarely witnessed in the States.

"John, you come from a land of abundance. Of plenty. Anything and everything you need is at your fingertips." Pastor Carlos contemplated. Searching for just the right words.

"Here, Jesus is all we have. We depend on Him for all things. For provision. For protection. For life itself. It is desperation. We are a people desperate for God. That is the difference!"

Chapter Ten

---≈---

John kissed Rachel's cheek, being careful not to wake her. He lingered for a few moments, enjoying her peaceful countenance. Then headed out for the early cattle sale.

An anniversary card was propped on her bedside table. Coffee was brewed. A slice of Rachel's favorite cream cheese Danish centered on an heirloom dessert plate. A napkin concealed the pastry.

Meet me at our favorite spot by the pond at 5 p.m. A grin enveloped John's face as he read the note that was taped to the steering wheel of his truck. Hearts were drawn all around and kisses applied in his wife's red lipstick.

John loved Rachel's little surprises. Today, he had a surprise for her. Three years had passed since they tied the knot. Since they gathered for a backyard wedding at the home of their neighbors and close friends, Tom and Helen Scott.

Rachel enjoyed her favorite breakfast in solitude. As she discarded the dishes in the sink, the memory emerged of the first homemade dinner she and John shared. Flirting over the soap suds. They made their home here. It only made sense.

Just as Rachel grabbed her keys to leave for work, there was a knock. She opened the door to a massive arrangement of daisies, lilies, and roses—a beautiful display of summer flowers. The card attached to the delivery read, *Happy Anniversary to the luckiest man alive and to the one who got away. Love you both!* Rachel laughed out loud. Jackson could always elicit that response from her.

She and John missed him. He was a source of joy they both needed. They had not seen him since the guys' annual mission trip one month earlier. Rachel had come to love the time John and Jackson spent together in the Amazon. She couldn't be prouder of the construction and agricultural work they were doing there.

Now that Jackson was working for his parents' construction company, his time spent in New Berry was limited to once a month. John and Rachel visited Georgia at least twice a year. Jackson was thrilled to host his best friends at the family home on Lake Lanier. John and Rachel prayed daily for Jackson to find a woman to love. They hated that he was alone. And so far away.

Rachel's day was split between farm chores and helping Uncle Jimmy out at the hardware store. Managing a farm and an inherited business kept him busy. The two broke away for lunch and Rachel's favorite gas station deli food, dumplings. They talked shop but mostly reminisced about the day he gave her away in a small garden with Mary, Martha, and Fran watching from above.

By quarter of five, Rachel was dolled up for her man. The beginnings of summer had already left shimmering highlights on her thick natural waves. Tanned skin accentuated her sky-blue eyes. The floral sundress hugged her figure.

Chanel, in all the right places, gave just the degree of sex appeal she desired. The packed picnic basket and blanket were loaded into the pickup. The temperatures of the June afternoon were perfectly moderate for her tiny feet, which remained bare.

A chilled bottle of muscadine juice was set on a tray with etched stems of crystal. The deepest red strawberries and chocolate kisses adorned dainty white pieces of the couple's wedding china. John's grandmother's patchwork quilt provided the perfect backdrop.

John approached the pond on the three-wheeler and drove toward the pickup. Five o'clock sharp. Rachel jumped from the blanket and greeted John for the first time of the day. He picked her up as they hugged and spun her around. "Happy Anniversary! I love you!" She dropped her chin and nuzzled her face against his chest, breathing in his Old Spice. "I love you too." There was no pretense. Just pure, young love.

The late-afternoon sun reflected off the water. Dragonflies flitted about. Light filtered through the leaves of the native laurel oak. The weather was beautiful, and the company perfect.

Rachel rolled her body toward her husband. She chose the most plump, juicy strawberry in the dish and dangled it over John's lips. Just as he attempted a bite, she pulled back. He turned his gaze to her playful grin. "Are you trying to start something? Because I'll take your dare!"

John reached over, grabbing Rachel's sides. Climbing onto her delicate frame, he began to tickle her body. Laughter rang out as well as her protests. She tried to wriggle loose, but he wasn't having it. They teased and wrestled and laughed until they cried.

"Gifts! Let's open gifts!" Rachel searched for a rescue. John relented, and the two settled down with a glass of refreshment. Rachel impatiently presented her gift to John. "You go first." He opened the box and pulled out a timepiece. An inscription on the back read, *Until the end of time.* "Very nice!" Adding the watch to his wrist, he investigated the features. Rachel looked on with pride.

"You will always know when it's time to come home to me." Rachel tilted her head and batted her eyes. One thing was for sure. John never stopped thinking of Rachel. There was no place he would rather be than right by her side. He leaned forward, kissing her forehead and offering his appreciation.

John reached under the edge of the blanket and retrieved a small box. There was no bow. Just the message *I love you!* written across the top.

Rachel shivered with excitement as she tore the paper away from the box. John was a self-proclaimed substandard shopper. But she never let him get away with his insecurity. Today, his efforts were spot-on.

Rachel opened the box with care, seeing that it was of a delicate nature. Her eyes engaged. She looked at John. Then the gift. And John again. He reached over, taking the box from her hands.

John removed the gift from its home. It dangled before her face. The late afternoon sun burst through the prism, casting a rainbow of colors in every direction.

"A diamond?" she asked as if she were not sure. "Yes. And the diamond is cut in the shape of a heart as a reminder that you will always have mine." Rachel was giddy. "I love it! Thank you!"

John unclasped the chain. Rachel reached back with one hand, taking hold of her hair and pulling it from her neck. Her eyes never left him. Reaching behind, he secured the clasp. The diamond shifted downward until it rested just above the curves of her cleavage.

Rachel took John's breath away. He leaned in to kiss her cheek. Her chin. Her earlobe. His breath grew heavier with every touch of his lips on her skin. With every response she gave.

Rachel tilted her head back, exposing the slender curve that transitioned down from her neck. John lowered the strap of her dress. He trailed his fingers with intention from the nape of her neck slowly to the crown of her shoulder and down her arm. A chill followed as her breath deepened.

Rachel turned her face to her husband's, guiding him inward toward her kiss. Pulling him to the blanket. Their passion ignited. Heart to heart. Completely.

The sun moved toward the horizon. The remaining light scattered the colors of the early evening into a soft pink that flooded the sky. Its splendor bounced off the floating cumuli almost like a dream. The lovebirds rested in their embrace.

A sound began to emerge from the solitude. John whispered, "It sounds like a horn blowing." Rachel sat up. "It IS a horn blowing!" The two jumped up from the blanket, readying themselves for unexpected guests. Clothes flew. Rachel giggled incessantly. John broke out in a sweat. He tipped over, attempting his trousers.

A red jeep could be seen in the distance making its way down the field road behind the trees. The horn continued to blow. As the vehicle approached, the couple could see it was their friends, Perry and Leigh Hastings. They knew how to make an entrance.

John and Rachel had known the two since late childhood. They were what Rachel called their *couple friends*. At least one night each weekend was spent sharing a meal and a movie. A movie that was rarely completed before two of the four began expelling low snores.

Leigh was a classic steel magnolia. Perry was sophisticated and debonair. Each was smarter than average. The four shared a common sense of humor and zest for life that ensured their time together was always refreshing.

"We aren't interrupting anything, are we?" Knowing smiles were cast toward the Averys. Perry nodded his head toward John, pointing out his misaligned buttons. "Not a thing!" John boasted with a sheepish grin as he attempted to correct the error in the most inconspicuous manner.

"You're still coming over tomorrow night for dinner, right?" Rachel affirmed. "We wouldn't miss it!" Leigh leaned in, giving Rachel a quick hug. "Great! See you about six. Happy Anniversary!" Perry extended a firm hand-shake to John, then turned for the jeep. "Don't do anything we wouldn't!" The friends exited as quickly as they entered, their horn blowing all the way.

John spun out on the three-wheeler. Rachel followed him to the barn. She scooted toward the middle of the bench seat, and John slipped in to drive. On the way back to Barton Manor, as the two liked to call their home, John detoured. "Where are we headed?" He didn't explain. "You'll see."

John turned onto an overgrown grass driveway at an abandoned home. The acreage he and his father had secured before his death. The place meant to grow John and Rachel's love and their family. It had been a while since the two had come here to dream.

John came to a stop at the old farmhouse that sat in the middle of a two-acre plot. In its prime of the 1920s, it was a jewel. The gabled front porch protruded toward the sunset. Its wooden swing, barely hanging by one remaining chain, reminded them that life had happened here. A good life.

Remnants were evident. Patches of heirloom petunias, purple and white, hugged the home's foundation. Crowded daylily crowns still birthed blooms of every variety among the neighboring weeds. A grand fig tree overtook most of the clothesline.

Staring forward, John took Rachel's hand. "One day, Rachel, we will make this our home. Our family will know the security of these rooms. The comfort of the front porch. The peace of the summer breeze moving through the pecan branches. Once, there was life on this homestead. There will be again."

Rachel basked in the enthusiasm of John's dreams. They were her dreams, too. "It all sounds divine. We could get started on the family tonight." She winked and pursed her lips, sending a kiss through the warm air.

John squeezed Rachel's body into his as the scent of honeysuckle drifted through the windows. "We might not be ready for the family just yet, but I do believe practice makes perfect."

John and Rachel arrived at the Hastings starter home right on time. As they approached, it was certain they were entering an already heated discussion. They followed the brick path around the home to the backyard.

"You two alright?" Perry and Leigh turned with looks of exasperation. They saw their friends and burst out in laughter. "*The Case of the Missing Grill.* I think Agatha Christie wrote it. Perry loaned out the grill a few months ago and doesn't remember to whom! No grill! No grilled steaks!"

Leigh and Rachel headed inside to evaluate the options. Before they could make any decisions, the guys yelled from the yard. "Problem solved!" The ladies peaked out to see Perry and John digging a small hole. "Grab the oven rack and the charcoal." The steaks on the makeshift grill were the best they ever had. Friends find a way.

The couples relaxed in the den with John and Rachel's wedding album. Perry and Leigh were quiet. Serious. "We have something to tell you." Perry couldn't hold back. He blurted out the news. "We're going to have a baby!" John and Rachel jumped to their feet and embraced their friends, who were more like family. "We couldn't be happier!"

"There must be something in the water!" Pastor Stephens started Sunday's service with a statement that couldn't be more true. Rachel and Leigh shared a glance and a smile. Nine couples in the church had announced pregnancies in the last three months. The pastor teased at their joyful predicament. "We'll grow this church one way or the other!"

The day for Rachel's annual appointment had arrived. The dreaded gynecology event. There was no getting around it. Not for her, nor for the rest of womankind. She had seen Dr. Mitch a few times in the past for unexplained pelvic pain. Even though this was a routine checkup, the pain discussion always surfaced.

The exam was the same each time. It was awkward, to say the least. Dr. Mitch stood over Rachel, examining her. His nurse was by his side. Rachel counted the ceiling tiles, praying for the seconds to pass. She was thankful when the exam was over and the doctor and nurse vacated the room.

Rachel took a moment to dress and regain her composure. Then headed to join Dr. Mitch in his office. His comments were abrupt. "Rachel, I think we are looking at endometriosis." After years of pain, his assessment made sense. "My suggestion. If you and John want children, you need to start trying right away. Getting pregnant might be an issue for you." Rachel was caught off guard.

"If you can get pregnant, the occurrence of the scar tissue will be reduced. Less menstrual cycles. Less scar tissue. Do you have any questions?" Doubt and fear came crashing in on Rachel. She couldn't think past his words. Much less ask questions. *Trouble getting pregnant? Lord, this can't be! What-ifs* moved to the forefront of her mind.

Rachel headed straight for Tom and Helen Scott's house. Helen was her friend and Sunday school teacher. A nurse by profession. Tom and Helen were loyal friends. It was late afternoon. Rachel found Helen working in her garden. The same intimate garden where she and John made their vows. They sat in the green solace while the full report was shared, along with the fear that accompanied it.

"No! That is not the report we are going to receive. Let's pray right now." In the moments Rachel needed it most, a powerful prayer that revisited the faithfulness of God throughout her life went forth. God met Rachel there. She remembered His assurances for her future. She was thankful for a place of encouragement. As the leaves swayed with the breeze, she felt God's Spirit moving within her. She remembered Romans 8:28.

With renewed hope and confidence, Rachel set out for the farm. She found John at the barn. She shared the events of the day. They held each other. God held them both.

It was only three months before Rachel and John were sitting on the side of the tub, staring at a tiny window on a wand, hoping for a blue sign that would bring a celebration. When the affirmative sign manifested on the pregnancy test, Rachel turned to John and fell into his arms. The doctor had been wrong.

Rachel couldn't wait to share the news. She was number ten. Ten women in a small church were pregnant. Ten friends sharing the sweet moments in life. After Mrs. Avery and Kaye, Jackson got the call. "Call me Uncle Jackson!" He was elated. Uncle Jimmy cried. After all his years alone, he was going to stand in as Grandpa.

There was so much happiness in the community. Nothing like babies— lots of babies—to spread joy. Every occasion of gathering found expectant mothers buzzing with stories of their pregnancy journey. Nausea. Weight gain. Cravings. Baby showers were set. A jolt of life hit New Berry.

Rachel was glad to have a place among the expectant mothers. While she and John waited to see the obstetrician, questionnaires were completed. Second trimester. Fourteen weeks. No current side effects were noted.

Dr. Mack ordered an ultrasound. "Let's get an early look. Just as a precaution. I'll send the order to the hospital right now." The couple was overjoyed for the opportunity.

Rachel readied herself on the table, struggling to maneuver the gown. The ultrasound technician, Fay, talked as she worked. She was full of personality. Keeping Rachel engaged in conversation. The procedure was hardly underway when Fay stopped. The monitor was turned away from the couple. She excused herself from the room.

The sterile surroundings didn't defer the warmth of John and Rachel's love and anticipation. He rested his hand over hers, fingers locked in unity. The opposite hand stroked the strands around her face.

Fay reentered. "Dr. Ander, our radiologist, is on vacation. Dr. Hand, from Fort Redding, is covering. He is going to look at your images with me." The couple had no reason to object. The more professionals celebrating their sweet baby, the better.

Fay moved the probe over Rachel's still-flat abdomen. Moving easily over the gel in repeated strokes. Dr. Hand looked at the images for no more than thirty seconds. "No heartbeat. There's no baby there!" As quickly as he had entered, he was gone.

Fay was startled. Rachel gasped. Tears instantly flooded her cheeks. John grabbed Rachel, locking her in his embrace. Anger overtook him. Fay grabbed the phone and pressed an extension. She whispered for a moment and then called for Dr. Hand. He took the receiver.

Dr. Mack unleashed his professional wrath. John and Rachel could hear his protests and correction. Dr. Hand hung up and turned to the shocked couple. "I'm sorry for sharing out of turn." He vanished.

John cuddled Rachel on the sofa. The phone rang. They looked at one another, then at the phone on the kitchen wall. Neither wanted to answer, but Rachel bit the bullet.

"Hello." John stepped close enough to hear. "Rachel, this is Dr. Mack. I got the results of your blood test. It was the only way to know for sure if you were pregnant or had had a false pregnancy. The test was positive."

Rachel released a long, heavy sigh. John pulled her body to his, holding her in place. "I'm not sure when the baby died. Or why. Sometimes this happens with no explanation. I'm very sorry for your loss."

Chapter Eleven

───── ≈ ─────

The sun had risen and set since the painful news was delivered. Rachel lay in darkness. She just wanted to sleep. To forget. She could hear a faint conversation beyond the bedroom door. "Dr. Mack said Rachel's body needs to release the baby on its own. That is what's best for her body now—and later."

John entered the room and addressed his wife in a whisper. "Rachel, you have visitors. Are you ok with that?" She raised her eyes to meet his. Her expression didn't change. He joined Rachel on the bed, snuggling in close behind her and wrapping her like a child. He rubbed his fingers in long strokes through her hair. When he didn't know what to say or do, he knew that brought her comfort.

"Rachel, Uncle Jimmy and Jackson are here. Jackson came straight from Gainesville when I called him. Uncle Jimmy was here through the night. He's very worried about you." She gave a slight nod.

Jackson maneuvered into the bedroom with a vase of flowers and a bouquet of balloons large enough for a child's birthday party. He didn't know how not to overdo it. At least not when it came to the Averys. He centered the vase on the dresser and approached the bedside.

He opened his mouth a few times to speak but stopped short. Rachel lifted her eyes toward him. "I've never known you to be speechless." He attempted a smile. There was just too much concern for it to emerge. "I remembered. Gardenias." An expression resembling a smile emerged on Rachel's face. She nodded. "Good boy." Jackson and John shared a satisfying look. Jackson had the gift.

Uncle Jimmy came through the door, his face clad with tears. Eyes swollen. He looked at Rachel, then turned away. Placing a small box on the bed, he walked out of the room. His tender sobs faded as he exited the adjoining hallway.

His heart was broken for John and Rachel. He had walked a similar journey. This day took him back to a pain too great to remember. "I'm not leaving this time. Not until I know she is alright." Nearly two decades later, he still contended with shame.

The whole crew was an emotional wreck. All four held so much hope for the tiny one that had grown inside Rachel. Now their hope had nowhere to rest.

A few moments later, the Hastings and the Scotts arrived with dinner. They made arrangements in the kitchen, then joined the others in the bedroom. Jimmy stepped back inside the doorway, dropping his eyes to the floor.

Standing, John addressed the group. "You are our closest friends in the world. Thank you for joining with us to bear our burdens, our pain, and our disappointment. The Bible tells us, THIS is fulfilling the Law of Christ. We love you all."

Uncle Jimmy sat on the bed, taking Rachel's hand. Jackson placed a firm grip on John's shoulders. Perry, Leigh, Tom, and Helen joined hands along the foot of the bed. This was the way they handled life.

Rachel sat up, looking into each person's face. She was thankful that when she couldn't find the words to pray, others came alongside, praying for her. Holding her up.

As the prayers closed, the friends lingered in the stillness. Leigh began to hum. In a solemn tone, the words of a hymn emerged.

Tis so sweet to trust in Jesus.

Just to take Him at His Word

Just to rest upon His promise

Just to know thus sayeth the Lord.

The friends joined in the chorus. As the harmony was raised, a holy peace settled in the room and in Rachel's heart. For this moment, John was grateful.

The morning light filtered through the windows as John tiptoed back into the bedroom. Rachel awoke, remembering immediately her plight…and the previous night's blessing. *Friends.*

The box Uncle Jimmy deposited was at her bedside. She propped herself on her pillows and began to investigate. It had an aged appearance and a simple beauty.

John delivered a steaming cup of coffee in Rachel's favorite English porcelain cup. "Good morning, Sleepy Head. I thought you might be ready for this." He placed the cup on the table and leaned in for a soft kiss.

"Look what Uncle Jimmy left."

"Yes. I saw it. Open it." Rachel raised the hinged lid. A snug note was removed to reveal an ornate hairpiece. The clip was of aged silver, with rubies adorning both sides.

Rachel gasped. "It's stunning!"

Unfolding the note, she read.

Rachel,

You share the same birthday month with my Mary. I gave this hairpiece to her in the first year of our marriage. It belonged to my mother. Your grandmother, Maggie. She died when you were just a baby.

Mary loved this clip and wore it often. I want you to have it. She would want you to have it. I hope this will cheer your heart. All my love.

Uncle Jimmy

Rachel swallowed hard. She arose from the crumpled sheets and stood before the dresser mirror. A tear disappeared into the breast of her silk gown.

With great care and reverence, she gathered her hair. Twisting her long strands, she captured them with the precious gift just below her crown. A few loose locks rested around the curves of her neck.

She lingered, taking in the gravity of the moment. John stepped from behind, observing Rachel in the mirror. "I've never seen anything more fitting."

Four weeks passed. Rachel still carried the baby. Dr. Mack conceded that her body wouldn't release the remains of her child. "I need to do a medical procedure. A dilation and curettage. This will clear your uterus. Your body will be prepared for your next pregnancy. Rachel, the fact that your body refused to let go of the baby is a good sign for the future. You're strong. Your body knows it was created to be a mother. It's holding on with everything it has."

Closure was needed, but questions she never conceived were constantly at the forefront of Rachel's mind. *Does heaven have a special place for babies not born into this world? Would she know him when she got to heaven? Would she ever again feel the satisfaction of carrying a child in her womb? Was it God's will?*

Rachel's sleep was often full of dreams. Dreams of her baby gone prematurely. A baby boy, she was sure. The image of his father. Handsome. Pale hair. Olive skin. John Avery, the Third.

Baby showers filled the calendar. Rachel volunteered for the first. It was delightful. Baby bumps abounded. Cheer was in the air. Rachel ensured a smile was constantly on her face as she and dozens of other women milled about the room.

"We don't know why God does what He does. He knows best, Rachel. He might have needed a special flower in His garden or another cherub for the choir." Rachel's eyes widened. Her face turned the brightest shade of red. Her body bowed up in defense.

"With all due respect, Ms. Carter, I don't believe—" Rachel's words were cut short as Helen scooped her away from a sure catastrophe. "Gotta get our piece of cake and punch before it's all gone." Rachel pulled away. "Hey, I was in a conversation with…with that…THAT WOMAN!"

Helen tilted her head and gave her a questioning look. "Do you really think you're going to change THAT? Do you think she is going to hear your point of view?"

Rachel relaxed her shoulders…and her attitude. "No! Thanks for the save." She dropped her head, concealing her amusement. "I'd hate to do something I would regret…right here in the fellowship hall."

Leigh approached the two. "I heard what was going down. I just couldn't get there to intervene. Good reaction time, Helen!" They shared a good laugh, thinking of the possible outcome.

The first celebration had passed. Rachel made it through. There were eight more showers to go. She wanted desperately to share in her friends' joy. To celebrate with them. She would not allow her sadness to overshadow even one.

As Rachel pulled into the driveway, John met her. He knew the baby shower would be difficult. But he would have needed to tie her down to keep her away.

"How did it go?" Rachel's laughter surprised him.

"Ms. Carter came out of it unscathed. I guess that's positive." John had no idea what that meant. He just listened.

"People just need to say they are sorry for your pain. For what you are going through. Instead of trying to give insensitive or inaccurate explanations for things they don't understand."

John nodded. "Oh, I get it. You are so right. I learned a lot about what NOT to say when my dad died. Most people were kind and sensitive. However, there was the occasional self-appointed philosopher who would make a comment that somehow made me feel worse. I am much more careful now when I encounter someone who is hurting."

John ushered Rachel into the den. He had a pillow and blanket ready for her on the sofa. "Get cozy. I'll bring you a dinner tray." Rachel was thankful for the way John anticipated her needs before she even knew them herself. He reentered with a bowl of his famous chili.

Rachel closed her eyes, trying to compose her thoughts. "I've learned a great deal from our loss. There was so much I didn't know before our baby left. I couldn't understand until the experience came to our home…to our life.

"I didn't know how my heart could be so broken for a child I never met. A baby whose body was fully formed but only big enough to fit in the palm of my hand. A baby talked about in Psalm 139 who was knitted together in MY womb.

"How a longing to hold him would consume me. How the curiosity to know his features would find me exploring the faces of little boys in the crowd. Oh, to feel his skin against mine. To inhale his sweet scent."

John joined Rachel on the sofa, guiding her body to lean into him.

"It seems that the world, in general, doesn't validate miscarriage as worthy of great sorrow or grief. I think of the women who came before me. Those I dismissed shortly after their loss, not thinking their experience or pain could linger."

John took Rachel's hands in his and offered a prayer. "Lord, we thank you for our sweet baby. We are grateful for the hope we hold through you that we will see him one day. We acknowledge Romans 8:28, which says that you are working all things for good. We anticipate with great excitement the little Averys to come. The family you will build. The life we will share." As the *amen* closed John's prayer, Rachel's heart was consoled.

Life returned to normal for the Averys. Right on schedule, John arrived at home at twelve o'clock sharp. Lunch was on the table. He greeted Rachel with an especially tight hug, which she enjoyed. John removed a document from his jacket pocket. He looked at it, biting his bottom lip. Holding it in both hands, he placed it on the table and slid it across to Rachel. "What's this?" John waited as Rachel unfolded the papers. *Paid in full* was stamped across the page.

Rachel jumped up, grabbing her husband around the neck. "The farm debt is paid! John, that's amazing! In just three years! Your father would be so proud of you!" John smiled, but Rachel knew there was more. "What are you not telling me?"

John sat. His nervousness could not be disguised. "Rachel, I've been thinking about the week I spent in the hospital at Health Center South. The spring after Dad died." Rachel nodded. "I remember. I will never forget that time. Ten days straight without keeping a single meal down. You being tested for colon cancer."

"Anxiety. It almost shut me down. The promise I made to my father has haunted me. Every day. The debt. The gamble each year that farming brings. My mother's future." Tears filled his eyes. "I love God. I really do trust Him.

I just can't get past this. I've tried. I hope you will forgive me for making these decisions alone. I felt I had to do what was best for everyone." Rachel was trying to understand. John wasn't making sense.

"I've sold the equipment to Uncle Jimmy. The proceeds from the sale made up the remainder of the loan payoff. He will begin leasing the land immediately. That will ensure my mom earns a guaranteed land rent payment each year. The same amount regardless of how the crops perform. She and Kaye will have a home with no encumberments."

Rachel was shocked. "John, farming is your life! What are you going to do?" John straightened his body with confidence. "Uncle Jimmy has asked me to manage Barton Hardware. He wants to expand farm support. I know it like the back of my hand. It's a win-win."

While Rachel was still processing the revelation, Uncle Jimmy leaned around the door frame. "Is it all clear?" Rachel snickered. "Yes, Uncle Jimmy. Come in."

He walked to the table, extending his hand to John with a firm handshake. Then he stepped behind Rachel. Wrapping his arms around her, he gave her a squeeze. "Anybody ever tell you that you have pretty eyes?" A smile emerged on Rachel's face.

"John had some tough decisions to make. I'm so proud of him." Rachel nodded, trying to hold back tears. John now carried a look of relief.

"John, any time you miss farming, just find a tractor and get busy. You will have the best of both worlds. I love you both and am honored to be a part of your lives. I'll support you any way I can."

"I guess since we're sharing news, I'll join in." Uncle Jimmy and John turned their heads with intrigue toward Rachel. "What is it? Is everything ok?" John knelt in front of his wife. His concern was undeniable.

"Yes. Everything is more than fine. It's been four months since the D&C." John straightened up. Uncle Jimmy held his breath. "I went to Dr. Mack yesterday for a blood test.

"Uncle Jimmy, since you're willing to support us any way you can, we'll be needing a babysitter." An all-encompassing smile covered Rachel's face. John and Uncle Jimmy cheered.

John and Rachel's world was shifting. Change had come once more. They didn't know exactly what the future looked like. But they knew that if they had each other and God, they could face anything.

Chapter Twelve

---≋---

Jackson straightened the paperwork that covered his desk. He was in a rush. There were work orders and purchase orders a plenty. Tasks that needed Monday morning attention were stacked on top of his *to-do* pile, a pile that was never eliminated. Never complete.

On any given day, there were multiple projects in the pipe. Additions, remodels, updates, and repairs. Emory University Hospital was ever-growing and changing. Adapting to the needs of the citizens of metropolitan Atlanta and surrounding counties and states, Jackson's role as construction manager kept him busy all day, every day.

This Friday afternoon, it all came to a halt. At least his part. He handed over the reins of each project to the next in command for the weekend. His sixteen-year-old namesake wouldn't have her Uncle Jackson miss her birthday party.

"Mrs. Smith, I'm headed out. I have to pick up my *surprise* for the party." He swung his head around the doorway into his secretary's office, offering a quirky grin. She tilted her head forward, looking over her bifocals. "Mr.

Stone, I hope everything goes well. My fingers are crossed. Give the Averys my love." John saluted. "Absolutely! Say a prayer!"

As Jackson disappeared from the office, Mrs. Smith's look turned grim. She had watched carefully over the last three months. She was uncertain whether the boss she admired and respected was taking the right path.

Jackson Stone was somewhat of a son to her. She had been sitting in her current position for more years than he had been alive. They spent their days in adjoining offices for the last decade of that service. Even if he visited her for advice, discernment was at the forefront. Staying in her lane took wisdom. She truly wanted what was best.

Jackson's F350 seemed to know the way to New Berry without much assistance from him. Securing the *surprise,* he pointed his truck toward the southwest and hit cruise control. Atlanta's rush hour didn't deter his monthly weekend trips to his home away from home. Though recently, trips were fewer. He couldn't wait to cross the state line.

Jackson was a true Atlanta city boy. Born and raised. His Huffy saw many adventures through the hills and valleys of his subdivision, edged next to the industrial park. Peachtree Street and Grant Park were his stomping grounds in the early years, when worldly dangers were still at arm's length. He would wander wherever his banana seat led.

The young Stone stayed out of serious trouble most days. On a Tuesday morning of his third-grade year, he diverted. Mr. Stone was called off the job site. Jackson and a few buddies traded the classroom for the excitement of downtown skyscrapers. A ten-cent fare got the tiny scoundrels to the middle of the action. The entire morning was spent among hotels, testing as many elevators as possible. Bottom to top and back again. Over and over.

It was at the Hyatt Regency that their luck went south. "It wasn't my idea," Jackson assured his father. As if that fact lessened the severity of his actions. The whole episode was born out of a dare. And Jackson Stone could not pass up a dare.

Mr. Stone had a heart-to-heart with his only child over a burger at The Varsity. Then dispensed the punishment. One month without his coveted Huffy. Even as an adult, Jackson would profess that it was absolutely worth the punishment. But never in the presence of his father. Regardless of Jackson's shenanigans, Mr. Stone always referred to his son as a *good boy*. Good, yes. However, he was the epitome of mischief.

The Stones were devout Christians. Sundays and Wednesdays would find them on the third row of Park Avenue Church, with Jackson wedged between father and mother. Family and friends were enlisted to help keep tabs on the rambunctious child. It took them all. Adult supervision was ensured during services. At the request of the pastor, Jackson wasn't often released alone—even to the restroom.

A Sunday morning of distraction found Jackson venturing into a tiny utility door in the hallway. In his Sunday best, he crawled through the long, narrow opening until he emerged from a second door. In the sanctuary. Just below the baptismal. Patsy Stone let out a horrific gasp just about the time Jackson's eyes met hers.

"Let us pray!" The pastor spoke to the deity just long enough to give Lane Stone ample time to retrieve his offspring from the pulpit platform. The *amen* resounded when Jackson was secured in his assigned position. A fellowship dinner at Park Avenue was rarely held without Jackson's mishap being revisited. Even as an adult, his moments of madness followed him.

Church was the site of many a calamity for the lanky young man, who was six-five by the time he was thirteen years old. Mrs. Stone often shook her head, wondering how her son could find so much mischief. Torn pants, grass stains, church yard skirmishes, broken windows. He kept his parents on their toes.

Jackson was full to the brim with personality. "He can charm the skin off a snake," Mr. Stone bragged with endearment. But it was the young man's heart of gold that always earned a greater helping of grace than most.

The latter years of Jackson's childhood were spent on the waters of Lake Lanier beyond Buford Dam. The purchase of a lot on the newly developed waterway was a dream. Stone Construction moved its office from Atlanta to Gainesville. Life became simpler.

Jackson and his father built a family home along with their crew. Mr. Stone imparted his skills, talents, and knowledge to his son. A blessed gift. Watching the two she loved most work side by side filled Mrs. Stone's cup. The family of three settled in.

Jackson was a social creature. Though he rarely dated. He stayed busy with school, friends, and the youth group. Making the most of lake life and mission work.

Missions had always been a priority for the Stones. Patsy's father and mother were full-time missionaries in Tanzania. She learned the power of serving in real time. Sacrifice was a part of her entire upbringing.

Lane Stone's experiences were much more traditional. He learned his trade at his father's side. Construction made a good living on the weekdays. Mr. Stone, the elder, and Lane often used their Saturdays and their talents to serve the widows and the community. Making repairs. Patching roofs. Building ramps. All in the name of Jesus.

In truth, both Lane and Patsy were missionaries in their own rights.

Jackson's lineage was steeped in Christianity. But he took ownership at a makeshift altar in a village deep in the Peruvian jungle when he was fifteen. The words of the pastor held limited meaning in the foreign language that he had yet to learn. Jackson came face-to-face with the Holy Spirit, who spoke the language of his heart. He surrendered to the Savior with Jimmy Browning by his side.

Jimmy Browning. His uncle by choice. And New Berry. His hometown of choice. Both opened a new world for the young man. A world far from the city life he knew best.

"Get ready for a *surprise*." Uncle Jimmy sounded almost amused. "What? What do you mean?" Rachel's mind was distracted with party details. "Hey! Did Jackson make it in safely last night?" She darted through the kitchen, searching for serving trays, her phone perched between her shoulder and cheek. "Oh, yeah! He made it in. Safe and sound."

"Jackson mentioned to John that he might bring a friend. The more, the merrier." Rachel giggled. "Actually, I'm glad he's got some friends besides us. Right?" Uncle Jimmy forced a laugh. "Rrriight."

"Is there anything you need from us? Can we pick up anything?" Rachel went through her mental list. "Ice. Please pick up a few bags of ice. Thank you! I can't wait to see you guys. Two o'clock sharp!"

By party time, cars had started lining the driveway and the edge of the adjoining field. Rowdy teenagers filled the backyard. Appetites intact. There was much squealing and running about. Most of the youth group was represented.

Gifts were displayed in the designated area with mylars in every shade of purple. Pizza, chicken wings, burgers, and chips and dip layered on a tablecloth in yet another purple design. This was teenage girl heaven.

Rachel stopped in her tracks when the birthday girl emerged from the house. She watched the debut from across the patio as friends rushed in. "John, how did this happen? Our Jacqueline. Sixteen years old. How is our first-born already sixteen?"

The two basked in the moment. They watched in awe as their three door-steps laughed and smiled among their friends. "Life happens, Rachel." He reached down, taking her hand, with his gaze still locked on his daughters.

"Isn't it beautiful! God is so, so faithful! I love our family of five. And being the only guy…well, I'm honored."

Rachel turned to her husband grabbing his cheeks between her thumb and pointer. She planted a kiss on his puckered lips, then went right back to work. As Rachel and Mrs. Avery tended to the last details, Jackson's truck pulled up the field road to the edge of the backyard. Uncle Jimmy jumped from the back seat, heading to the house with bags of ice. The uncles were normally early. On time for them meant late.

Jackson stood at the passenger door. "What is he doing?" Rachel shot John a confusing look. "He brought a *friend*, remember? Surprise!" As Jackson held the door, the *surprise* came into view. Rachel's jaw dropped.

She was stunning. Every bit of five-ten. Mostly legs—long and slender. Accentuated by five-inch heels found at the ends of her flawless designer jeans. Her skin was perfect. Reflecting a glow from her white silk blouse. Her makeup no less than professional quality. Straight, jet-black hair hugged her back. Every strand in place. It waved in sync as the couple approached their hosts. Rachel shook herself from the trance of disbelief.

"Sorry we're late. She had to finish her hair!" Uncle Jimmy raised an eyebrow as he dropped the ice bags. "Sorry, Rachel. Jackson wanted you to be surprised." She raised a thumbs-up. "Accomplished!"

"Rachel. John. I'd like for you to meet Anastasia." Rachel smiled and stepped forward to greet her guest. There was an awkward play of hands before Rachel retreated. "We are so glad you joined us for Jacq's birthday." John nodded. "Yes, welcome! Any friend of Jackson is a friend of ours."

"Thank you. It's nice to finally see the place he never stops talking about." She glanced at Jackson, who carried a satisfying grin. "Can I get you a soft drink?" John leaned over, opening the ice chest. "No, thank you, Mr. Avery." The host affirmed, "Please call me John."

Arms converged on Jackson's waist from behind. He laughed out loud. "Now I wonder who that could be?" Anastasia took a step back, avoiding contact. "Uncle Jackson! Where have you been? We've missed you!" Faith and Beth claimed ownership of their Uncle Jackson. Though there was no blood between them.

Jacq was a few steps behind her sisters. She stepped in front of them as an older sister would, wrapping her arms around Jackson's waist and squeezing. She looked up with her mama's eyes and cast a heartbreaker smile.

"Happy Birthday, Jacq! Do you know I was there on the afternoon you were born? You arrived with your eyes wide open." Jacq's cheeks were frozen in happiness. "Yes sir! You tell me every year." Jacq turned her body toward the unexpected guest. She looked up again at Jackson, inquiring. "Girls, I want you to meet my friend, Anastasia." He reached out, taking her hand, though she remained at a distance. "Thank you for coming to my party with Uncle Jackson. Isn't he the greatest?"

Anastasia was relieved when the festivities were over. She settled on Uncle Jimmy's sofa. "Why is the kid named after you?" Her look conveyed a hint that something was awry. "Anastasia, don't be crass. Her mom and dad have been my very best friends for twenty years. I was and am still honored beyond words. Isn't she beautiful?"

"Are you talking about the kid or the mom. They look just alike, you know." Jackson let out a rolling laugh. "You are so silly! Jacq! I was talking about Jacq!"

"Come on. Get changed into something casual. I want to show you around New Berry before it gets dark." Anastasia lounged on the sofa with a magazine. She rolled her head around to face Jackson, as if removing her eyes from the text was a bother. "I was really enjoying just sitting here catching up on my reading. And, by the way, this IS my casual."

"I'm hungry for chicken divan. Any five stars around here?" Jackson looked sternly at Anastasia. "Uh, no! Besides, we have dinner plans in a few hours. When Uncle Jimmy gets back from feeding the cows, we're loading up to go to our favorite steakhouse with the Averys. It's a quaint restaurant in an old church. The best certified Angus ribeye south of the Mason-Dixon. Homemade onion rings. I can already taste them. You'll love this place!"

"I'm sure!" Anastasia rolled her eyes. "Beef! Really?" She stood and approached Jackson. "For you! This is all for you!" She kissed his cheek, leaving her mark in bright red. "I'm sure I can find a suitable pasta dish on the menu." Jackson was amused at her misconception but chose to leave her thoughts uncorrected. The smirk on his face revealed his true mischievous bent.

"I'll be in my room until it's time to go." She disappeared.

Jackson remained in the den. Many seasons of his life were anchored in this very home. He strolled along the edge of the fireplace mantle. Years of photographs lined the solid beam. He paused in front of a hand-hewn wooden frame with a notation slipped inside at the edge of the glass. *Best Friends!*

Jackson and John stood on either side of Rachel. All arm in arm. An overused peanut wagon labeled with its numerical designation as their backdrop. Number Three. The last ton had just been secured at the buying point. Jeans and boots attired the three. Rachel's hair was a windblown mess. Peanut dust covered each from head to toe. They were so young.

The happiness of their achievement was memorialized in the laughter captured in one snapshot. It was the year they met.

Jackson lingered in the moment. More so in the memory. He could still smell the dust from the day. Feel the warm breeze that swept across the empty field. Most importantly, his heart remembered the excitement for friendship found. Friendship for a lifetime.

Chapter Thirteen

T he daffodils had scarcely begun to bloom when a new season of life
emerged. John and Rachel received the call. Emotions were high. The
couple had anticipated this day. Even prayed for it. When it arrived, their
hearts were unexpectedly quiet.

"I've asked Anastasia to marry me!" Jackson's whoop echoed through the
receiver. "She said yes! She actually said yes!" We're getting married in June,
when hydrangeas are at their peak! She loves hydrangeas! White hydrangeas!
Have I said that already?" Jackson's explosive excitement was contagious.
Even over speakerphone.

The three friends began to laugh. When Jackson was happy, there was
no containing the joyful fire that ignited around him. This was one quality
of which John and Rachel couldn't get enough.

"Jackson! We are thrilled for you!"

"Yeah, man! Congratulations!"

"We just want you to be happy."

"I *AM*! I thought I was happy alone. Now, I have a glimpse of what I've been missing. I need my best friends by my side for the most important day of my life."

Rachel looked into John's face with painful resolve. It seemed they were at the end of an era as another gave way.

New Berry was abuzz with excitement for Jackson. Though not officially from the small town, he had been grafted in as a favorite son. He had been present for as much life as anyone. Present for the ups and downs of so many who called New Berry home.

Each Avery family member was assigned to serve at the wedding. Rachel would be a bridesmaid at Jackson's insistence. Jacq, Faith, and Beth, junior bridesmaids. John, of course, was slated to stand as best man.

With each having a wedding assignment, Aunt Kaye was recruited to help. Her new life made it a challenge. But she couldn't wait to see Jackson say, "I do!" The travel would be worth it.

Kaye was now Mrs. Anderson. She had wed Tucker Anderson shortly after John and Rachel's second doorstep, Faith, was born. The couple had a burning desire to translate years of short-term missions experience into full-time ministry.

After Mrs. Avery's death, they moved their lives across the equator. The jungle villages they had come to love over the past twenty years became home. Kaye's teaching degree and Tucker's medical training made them the perfect pair to serve the needs of the rural Peruvian communities. The last three months proved just that.

Their flight from Lima to Atlanta was right on time.

The Averys awoke to an Eastern Zone sunrise. They lingered over their in-room breakfast. Compliments of the groom. The Marriott Marquis served scrumptious French toast with warm maple syrup. A family favorite.

As the last bites were swallowed, the girls scattered for the shower, makeup mirror, and flat irons in their adjoining room. John and Rachel soaked up a few more moments with hot coffee. It was difficult to pull themselves away from the unobstructed view of the city.

Rachel broke the silence. "I want Jackson to be loved as deeply as he loves. He deserves that." John nodded in agreement but added nothing to the sentiment. John and Rachel had not found peace in this circumstance. Yet. Of course, it was Jackson's life. Not theirs.

Anastasia came from money. The family's primary home was nestled in Buckhead's elite Tuxedo Park. The monstrosity of a home was the norm for Dr. Blevins and his family. The hustle and bustle of Atlanta life seemed far away from their doorsteps. The long, winding driveway beyond the locked gate ensured not only protection but also privacy in the Blevins' life of solitude.

Anastasia's father was a renowned cardiothoracic surgeon at Emory University Hospital. Being in close proximity to the facility was necessary. Dr. Blevins was a brilliant man. He loved his work. His family. And his weekly tee time.

Mrs. Blevins volunteered throughout the week with various charities. On Thursday afternoons, she spent a few hours reading to children at Emory's Ingram Burn Center. The remainder of her time was given to numerous non-profits.

The family's weekends were spent at their home at Lake Lanier's premier Harbour Point. The exclusive gated community was an elite statement of success. Its grandeur was unmatched. The emergency helipad in the backyard proved just that. Jackson's family home was located a few miles away on the other side of the same lake. Two worlds unto their own.

Anastasia's passion was art. She thrived on the intellectual stimulation of its details. The artists. The time periods. The architecture. It was clean. Precise. Quiet. Upon her graduation from Emory University, Dr. Blevins purchased an existing gallery as a gift for his daughter. Anastasia's Master of Art History degree was immediately utilized. The gallery, along with its newly renovated studio apartment, existed just minutes from the Buckhead home. There, a suite was maintained for her special use. To encourage visits.

On occasion, Mrs. Blevins insisted that Anastasia venture beyond the inanimate world of art and interact with people. It was on a day when she chose not to object to her mother's prodding that her path crossed with that of a charming gentleman in a yellow hard hat. Jackson stopped in his tracks when he heard an angelic voice coming from the room of a five-year-old burn victim. He peaked in the doorway.

The tiny patient giggled when the tall man began to recite *Brown Bear, Brown Bear, What Do You See?* with its reader. Her parents invited him in. Anastasia was captivated.

A decade stood between the construction manager and the gallery owner. If opposites attracting was the indicator of a successful start, they were a perfect fit. The self-declared bachelor was bitten. Just months away from his forty-second birthday, he would be tying the knot.

Jackson's request for a New Berry wedding was not entertained. Anastasia didn't share his history there or his love for the small community. Her upscale world seemed much further away than the four-hour drive. Anastasia could not fathom what motivated Jackson to drive to New Berry each month. She couldn't comprehend his level of friendship with the Averys. His commitment to Jimmy Browning.

She was content in her small portion of Georgia. Her studio apartment over the gallery met all of her needs and wants. She was content. She tolerated Jackson's need for his life in the adjoining state. For now. As a matter of record, for her, it was all too much. Jackson's blind love for his future bride wouldn't allow him to doubt her or her intentions.

Summer hadn't come fast enough for Jackson. Now it had arrived in all its glory, along with his bride's favorite white hydrangeas. The season's sunshine arose on his long-awaited day. Jackson awoke in a blissful fog. *Wedding Day.*

The Averys arrived from the hotel dressed and ready. Rachel turned the girls over to Aunt Kaye, then began to seek out directives from the wedding planner. As she approached the intersection of walkways in the church courtyard, she heard her name. "I always thought Jackson would find a girl like Rachel." Before she could stop her body's motion, Rachel crossed into an opening and was standing in the presence of Mrs. Stone and Ms. Smith. Mrs. Stone's face held lingering evidence of her sobs.

The ladies portrayed a look of shock when, in that very moment of conversation, Rachel appeared. "Oh my, Rachel! I'm so embarrassed about what I said! I simply meant that I hoped Jackson would find someone more like him. Someone to love…like he loves you. Uh, uh."

The more Mrs. Stone tried to speak, to clarify, the bigger the mess of words became. With every attempt, Rachel grew more horrified. She couldn't speak.

Mrs. Stone broke down in tears. She rushed away. Ms. Smith remained. "Rachel, Patsy and I have been friends since college. I have a special relationship with Jackson. I recommended him for his job at Emory. He had to be incredibly experienced and equipped to do the job, of course. I have been with him for ten years. Patsy and I have prayed for Jackson's future since his birth. He is such a good soul. He loves big. We simply want him to be loved the way he loves.

"We thought someone LIKE you would be a better match for him. In all of his life, he was happiest with you and John. Patsy and I are so thankful for the two of you." Ms. Smith's eyes began to tear. "Anastasia is different. Not bad. Just different. It just seems that the love…the giving, is often one sided." Rachel lifted her head. Those exact words explained her heart in the matter. Her mixed emotions made perfect sense.

Rachel located Mrs. Stone in a back pew of the church. No one questioned her tears. After all, her only child would be married before the sun set on this day. "Oh, Rachel, that all sounded awful. I'm so embarrassed!" Rachel gave Mrs. Stone a gentle hug. "Don't be. I understand a mother's love." She leaned into Rachel as her tears continued.

Rachel found a prayer room and knelt in the solitude.

Lord,

My heart is so heavy. Am I being selfish? John and I have had Jackson's undivided friendship for years. We're afraid of losing him. We want him to be happy. To love. To be loved. I give this to you. I can't carry it. Please help me deal with my doubts.

Rachel lingered. The soothing instrumental of *It Is Well* calmed her heart. In this moment, she could feel the warmth of God's love.

A slow creak broke the solace. She turned to see Mrs. Blevins standing in the doorway. "I didn't want to disturb your prayer time. It's hard to find a place this conducive away from all the distractions." Rachel stood. "Yes, ma'am."

"Anastasia asked me to find you. She would like to visit with you in these last few moments before the ceremony. If you are ready now, I'll take you to the bridal suite." Rachel followed through the maze of hallways of St. Luke's. Though there were questions about Anastasia's intent in calling for her, she was calm.

Rachel gave a gentle knock on the intricately carved door. She entered the most beautiful room she had ever seen. It looked as if a princess might emerge. An ornate chandelier with a thousand delicate crystals caught every ray of light remaining in the early evening sky. Layers of handmade moldings defined the grandeur of the space. Majestic windows adorned with ceiling-to-floor upholstered drapes welcomed lavish garden views.

The floor length mirror embellished with twelve-inch gold framing dominated the east-facing wall. Pristine period seating lavished in deep blue velvet would have welcomed the likes of Queen Victoria. As Rachel basked in the splendor of the moment, a princess did, in fact, appear. Perfectly matching the setting. Rachel held her breath and the tears that rushed to her eyes.

She was speechless. She was sure no royal nuptials could surpass the elegance before her.

Ivory satin cascaded gentle shimmers of light along Anastasia's simple, sleeveless gown. Embracing her figure perfectly. A modest jewel neckline. Full-length ivory gloves.

Anastasia's olive skin was warm. Glowing. Her sleek black hair was wrapped in a chignon bun enclosed in pearl netting. From head to toe, she was flawless.

"Anastasia!" Rachel waited. She held her words. Would any words be sufficient? "You're stunning!" A gentle smile lightened Anastasia's cheeks. "Thank you, Rachel! That means a great deal coming from you. Come and sit with me."

Anastasia was not emotional. She portrayed confidence. Assurance. Strength. "I want to apologize." Rachel straightened up. Unsure of where the conversation was going. "Please hear me out. I've been jealous of your family, your church, your community. I have especially been jealous of you. Jackson has a history with all of you. Memories. Years of memories. He loves spending time in New Berry. He finds so much happiness there. I'm the new girl who doesn't seem to fit into a world that is already established."

Anastasia's eyes moved up and down Rachel's frame. "Jackson measures every woman by Rachel Avery. You are his standard. You are a hard act to follow. Rachel, why do you think he has been alone for so long? No one measured up to you!"

"Anastasia, I... I... I didn't know. I don't know what to say." Anastasia rested her hand over Rachel's. "It's ok. I know none of it was intentional. Jackson has always wanted what you and John have. He assumed he would only be happy with someone like you. Turns out, you and I are complete opposites. Despite that fact, he still fell in love with me."

An offensive note struck Rachel's heart. She waited. "I love Jackson. He loves me. Our love doesn't look like yours and John's. Jackson and I are opposite in many ways. Yet the same in the ways that matter. We have to forge our own path.

"Recently, I laid all my cards on the table. I gave him an opportunity to call it quits. If that was what he wanted. Just in case he wasn't sure. He chose me...again. Rachel, I'd like to ask that you and John pray for us. Pray that we can make a home. That we can live happily on the common ground." Rachel leaned in, lightly embracing Anastasia. "Absolutely!"

Before the conversation ended, the door opened. A half dozen brides-maids converged, along with three adorable juniors. The mother of the bride and Mrs. Stone were close behind. Rachel checked the details for each of her girls. Hair. Makeup. Dresses. She pulled on her full-length black gloves. Completing a three-sixty in the mirror, she was ready. They were ready.

The ladies stood in a circle around the bride. Every person was mesmer-ized. Royalty was no match. Anastasia drew the group's attention. "Rachel, would you pray? Please pray that God will bless these sacred moments and all the years to come." Rachel confirmed with a nod. "Heavenly Father...."

A room in the east corridor held Jackson, John, Uncle Jimmy, and the fathers. As the remaining groomsmen filed in, the room grew quiet. John looked at his best friend with the intent to speak. He couldn't. They exchanged a solemn grin, then submitted to a brotherly embrace. Both remained speech-less. Mr. Stone held back tears. They looked to Uncle Jimmy to pray.

Before the *amens* sounded, the historic church bells marked seven o'clock. Calling every person to the holy sacrament of marriage.

Chapter Fourteen

―――――≈―――――

The Stones' honeymoon was a month-long adventure. With the kind of money Anastasia came from, that was not unusual. Jackson used every day of vacation leave plus some. France was their destination. The destination of lovers.

A promised jolt to Normandy for the final weekend was negotiated for Jackson. Omaha Beach was a must. An overdue tribute would be paid there.

Jackson engaged in the excursions scheduled by his new bride. All the while fielding calls from Ms. Smith and contractors. Emory University Hospital stood still for no man.

Most days were spent on the French Riviera. Courtesy of Dr. and Mrs. Blevins. Luxury hotels with private beaches. Yacht clubs. And the best of fine dining each evening. They embraced the high life and spared no expense. Whatever made Anastasia happy brought the same to Jackson. Saint-Tropez, Monaco, Monte Carlo, Antibes, Versailles—each made her happier than its predecessor.

Every gallery. Every studio. Every cathedral had to be explored. Anastasia was driven to distraction. Jackson often allowed his bride to immerse herself in her passion. As her solitude most efficiently facilitated.

During his days, he took in the lighter side of their surroundings, which suited him. Not all artifacts of the past sparked his interest. Only those near and dear to his heart. He preferred living in the present.

Jackson had coffee among the locals. Engaging in conversations when English was an option. He was pleasantly surprised by the similarities between his Spanish and their French. Allowing for a greater understanding than expected.

He walked along streets off the beaten path. The places where French life was really lived. Where intimate family gardens were indulged at the end of a hard day's work. He laughed with preschool children playing silly games with their au pair. He loved the children. And they loved him.

Tourism held less allure for Jackson. He partook of local bistro cuisine with cooks who resembled a grand-ma-ma. Local artists painting far-reaching views caused him to linger. He breathed in the people. Their lives. And their stories. All the while missing his friends, who were a grand part of his own story.

A romantic train ride through the French Alps was Jackson and Anastasia's common ground. Though she was not impressed with the close quarters. A formal dinner served among ice-capped mountain views was a dream for these honeymooners.

Paris earned a dedicated week. Rachel defined the Louvre as her happy place without hesitation. The Mona Lisa didn't disappoint. Notre Dame's Gothic structure was a masterpiece that enthralled Jackson's architectural aptitude.

Their final stop…Normandy. Jackson was restless. His emotions were high. As a lad, he had sat on his grandfather's knee while stories were recited.

Grandpa Stone's voice quivered with each recollection of his beloved twin, Luke. He never wanted his memory to be lost.

"Luke was a card. He had a laugh that lit up the whole family. He could build anything. He loved people. *Lucius Jackson Stone*. Carry his name with honor."

The Stones had invested a most precious asset in the battle for freedom. Private First Class Lucius Stone stormed the beaches with many comrades on D. Day. The first wave. He was never seen again. Jackson vowed to one day stand on the beach that carried their brave soldier forever to the sea, a vow to his Grandpa Stone realized decades after his death.

Jackson led Anastasia to the *Walls of the Missing*. The magnitude of the moment held them in place. Draped in humility.

Stone, Lucius Pfc. was memorialized in granite, among many others. They stood in silence. In this place, there were no differences between them. Here, they were one.

In remembrance.

In gratitude.

Mr. and Mrs. Stone experienced the honeymoon of a lifetime, though tempered by disaggregation. Together, yet alone—a glimpse of the life to come.

Within days, Atlanta life returned to normal. Memories milled constantly in the minds of the newlyweds. Conversations kept the adventures fresh. The next event on the couple's calendar was Jackson's forty-second birthday. October seventeenth.

"I thought we might go to New Berry for my birthday this year. I haven't seen everyone since the wedding. It's been too long." Jackson waited and wondered how Anastasia would respond. He had come to expect disparities.

"I was thinking of dinner at Ruth's Chris Steak House with our parents. Since you prefer beef." She gave Jackson a sassy wink. His shoulders drooped. "Then a trip south for a few days to hang out with your friends. Surprise!" Jackson grabbed his wife's waist and pulled her close. "Thanks, Babe! You know me well! We can stay the whole weekend!"

"Actually, I meant you. While you're gone to New Berry, my mom and I are going to an art show in the Big Apple. I need some new inventory. And we can do some early Christmas shopping." More than anything, Jackson wanted his bride by his side, but he conceded.

Guests filed in. New Berry came out in record numbers. Jackson had touched many lives. Young and old. He took his stance in the assigned location near the barn entrance. The guest of honor was not allowed to do any work...per Rachel. Simply receive his birthday guests as instructed. Jackson had not anticipated a party, but seeing the community he loved was priceless.

For decades, Jackson invested in the community and the church. He contributed financially to those in need. Gave freely of his time and talents. No one would have ever known he was not born and raised on their soil. No good deed had been forgotten. Celebrating Jackson Stone was easy.

He never asked for anything in return. Jackson had inherited his parents' giving spirit. He loved through action. It was that exact benevolence that earned him best friend status in the life of John Avery. His only birthday request: no gifts. His friends had a way around his humility, however.

"Guys! This is amazing! Who knew the barn could be transformed into this? I'm honored. And Mom and Dad. I'm so glad you came. Thank you for making the trip." Mrs. Stone embraced her son. "We wouldn't have missed it."

Tables were lined end to end. Mismatched chairs filled every space along the long rows, accommodating the excess turnout. String lights hung by John cast a warm glow. A welcoming ambience. All looked and felt just as it should.

The meal was an unmatched Southern delight. Fried chicken was center stage, with every homemade side dish Jackson could imagine displayed. No birthday cake was needed. The ladies of First Community Church ensured Jackson had a surplus of all of his favorites. German Chocolate, Red Velvet, Key Lime, and many more. The food and the fellowship were the best gifts. All evening, Jackson felt loved and humbled.

Pastor Stephens stood. "As you know, the church sells bar-b-que plates twice a year to benefit the Agape Children's Home. A special thanks to John Avery and Jimmy Browning for donating the hogs. After the kitchen fire at the children's home last month, there was a budget shortfall. In honor of our friend, Jackson Stone, we collected an offering.

"I am happy to report that in one night, we collected three thousand dollars!" Everyone cheered, turning to Jackson for his response. His satisfaction was evident in his smile. "In addition, Jackson's in-laws, Dr. and Mrs. Blevins, sent word that they would match our donations. Our new total, six thousand dollars!" The room erupted.

"Finally, Jackson's parents, Lane and Patsy Stone, have also offered to match our collection." Pastor Stephens offered a nod of recognition toward the Stones. Mr. Stone pointed toward the heavens. "Our final total, nine thousand dollars! The affairs of the children's home are covered. Thank you all!"

It was a spectacular night for the beloved Jackson Stone. And the children of Agape, whom he loved.

The crowd had dispersed by ten o'clock. Jackson, along with his parents, Uncle Jimmy and the Averys, enjoyed the cool fall night from the back porch. A pot of coffee was shared among them.

Wedding stories were elicited. Pictures shared. Recollections of the great World War II memorial revisited. The night felt familiar. Like old times.

Jacq, Faith and Beth sat among friends. The campfire at the edge of the yard was in clear view from the porch. Several boys a little older than Jacq were among those who surrounded the fire. Of the nine women who gave birth before Rachel's rainbow baby, all nine had boys.

The adults talked about the odds of one hundred percent of the babies born in the church that year being male. Then came little Jacq. A sweet flower among the rough and tumbles. Rachel leaned in, looking toward Jackson.

"When should we expect a Stone baby? You two don't need to waste any time. I am ready to be Auntie Rachel." Rachel snapped her fingers and laughed out loud. "Tick tock!" Mrs. Stone dropped her coffee cup. She scurried to clean up the mess. Mr. Stone arose to assist his wife.

Jackson dropped his head. "How were the peanuts this year? First New Berry harvest I've missed in twenty years." Rachel cast a confused glance among her guests. The abrupt subject change was odd. The avoidance was uncharacteristic.

"Little less per acre than last year, but no complaints. Right, Uncle Jimmy?" Rachel could sense the tension. "What? What is going on? Why is everyone acting so suspicious? What am I missing? Mrs. Patsy?" Mrs. Stone immediately began to cry, as if she had been desperately trying to hold back. She excused herself to the kitchen. Jackson avoided eye contact with Rachel. He squirmed like a child about to offer a confession but fearing repercussions.

"Mr. Lane?" He looked at the floor and made no effort to respond to Rachel. "WHAT is going on? John? Uncle Jimmy?" Jackson stood attempting to take control. "Stop! Rachel, I am so sorry we kept this from you. We knew you would be very upset."

"Is someone dying?" A look of terror dropped on Rachel's expression. She couldn't imagine what was going to be revealed. Why everyone in her circle felt it necessary to keep it from her.

"Rachel, let's take a walk." She glanced at John with doubt. He arose and accepted her into his embrace. "No one is dying. Jackson has something to tell you."

Jackson led Rachel to the swing in the side yard. The one he and John set in place for her shortly after the two wed. A place where many life struggles were resolved among friends. They sat in apprehension.

"Anastasia and I decided we wouldn't have children." Rachel stood to her feet and faced Jackson. "What? The two of you decided?" Rachel released a hesitant giggle, thinking Jackson was teasing. His look shut down the misconception.

"I don't understand. Do you mean she's unable to conceive?" She waited for Jackson's explanation. "No, Rachel. It's not like that. Ummm." Jackson searched for the least severe words. "We just agreed that we would take a different route."

"I have no idea what you're talking about! A different route? What does that even mean?" Her voice began to quiver. She could feel frustration building. "Jackson, be straight with me! Quit mincing words! What is this all about?"

Jackson leaned forward, pressing his face in his hands. "We made a decision together that we would not have children." Rachel shook her head. "No! You love children! For twenty years, that's all you have talked about. Stop this!"

Kneeling down in front of Jackson, she pleaded. "Just tell me the truth!" Jackson lifted his head. He was face-to-face with Rachel, his heart pounding. He never wanted to disappoint her.

"One week before the wedding, Anastasia came to me. She confessed that she didn't want children. She has never had the desire. Never had a bent toward motherhood. Ever!

"She knew that I had my heart set on a family. She came clean. She wanted me to know the truth. Then I could decide for myself if I wanted to call it quits or move forward with her." Rachel rose to her feet. She paced back and forth in front of Jackson. Anger quickly found its way to the surface. "Cards on the table! THAT'S what she meant! All of you kept this from me because you knew I would be angry! Because I SHOULD be angry! We should ALL be angry! Tears of disappointment and anger amalgamated in an outburst. "That...that wretched...!"

"Rachel! Don't! Yes, she should have told me from the beginning! The decision I had to make seven days before we were scheduled to say 'I do' was not fair! The fact that she let me go on and on about having children. Grandchildren for my mom and dad. It was wrong. I have always wanted... ALWAYS wanted..." Jackson couldn't go on. He broke.

He had not let himself feel the disappointment of his decision. The magnitude. The finality. Until now. Among the tears, his answer was clear. "Yes! I'm mad! I'm sad! I'm disappointed!

"But I had a choice!" His voice began to lower as he took control of his emotions. "I chose Anastasia! I love her!"

John approached. Only the dim light from the barn cast on the couple. Rachel turned and buried her face in his chest. Tears erupted again. Tears shed for a friend whose hope would be forever void.

Anastasia had, in fact, played her cards well. Rachel wondered if her motives would ever be clear. Had she manipulated their dear friend by withholding the truth until just the right time? Rachel wasn't sure she would ever be free from the contempt and resentment that were seeding in her heart.

"I love your kids. Jacq, Faith and Beth are like my own. I love them deeply. My parents love them. Being Uncle Jackson is enough."

"Anastasia doesn't love them!" John's face expressed his shock that Rachel was so blunt with Jackson. "She doesn't even like them. Do you think they can't tell? Do you think they can't feel when she steps away from them, avoiding contact?"

As soon as the words left her mouth, Rachel knew she was wrong. Her regret was instant and profound. Her words, though truthful, were like a knife to Jackson. She knew she had cut him deeply.

Rachel stepped back to the swing and sat next to her friend. She wrapped her arms around his crouching body and pulled him close. If only she could rewind the moment. If only she could go back and choose kindness.

"Oh Jackson! I'm so sorry. I'm so, so sorry!" She looked up at John, begging for his intervention. Her expression was pure desperation. John shrugged his shoulders. He could find no way to rescue her. The words were spoken and could not be taken back.

Jackson offered no response. This was a first. Rachel's heart was breaking. She had broken his. She arose from the swing, rubbing her fingers through Jackson's soft curls. She approached John. "I'm sorry." Her head rested for a few moments on his chest. Then she left the two to sort out the mess she had made.

Mrs. Stone was found in the gathering room with a box of tissue on her lap. "Rachel, I can't tell you how sorry I am for keeping this from you. We all knew Jackson needed to be the one to tell you. When he was ready. When you walked up on my conversation at the wedding, I was having a meltdown. Trying not to cause a scene. Trying to process my disappointment and anger as I saw the sun setting on Jackson's fatherhood. Hoping for the strength not to stand when the pastor asked if anyone had objections to the marriage."

Rachel smiled. "That would have been something!" Mrs. Stone giggled through her tears. Thankful for a lighter moment. "I know! Rachel, this is too big, too much for me to carry. My heart is broken for my son. For our family. I know God would not have me carry bitterness for my daughter-in-law. But in just four months, my heart is hard toward Anastasia."

"Mrs. Patsy, I am not innocent here. I'm so angry. I feel as though Anastasia has taken a precious gift from Jackson. From all of us. The void she has caused is unforgivable. I need God to do in me and through me what I cannot do for myself. Because right now, I hate her!"

Sunday morning service was an emotional struggle. The crew gathered at the Averys' for lunch afterwards. Jackson had requested Rachel's chicken and dumplings with homemade chicken salad. "It's still my birthday weekend!" He argued with boyish insistence. She gladly obliged, relieved that Jackson had not forever held her verbal indiscretions against her.

The mood was a bit lighter than the previous evening. All enjoyed the lunch. The fellowship. The final moments shared. Before the Stones headed north, Jackson invited Rachel for another walk. "Let's go back to the swing." John gave Rachel a gentle push in Jackson's direction. Jackson reached over, rubbing the top of Rachel's head, causing a complete mess of her Sunday hair. "Jackson!" He repeated the mischief against her objection. "Stop it! Still as aggravating as ever!"

He cast her a sincere smile. "What did you expect?" She gave in and submitted to a delightful laugh. Jackson simply wanted Rachel to be happy. Especially happy with him.

"Rachel, I thought I could make Anastasia love this place and the people as much as I do. I realize now that I was not realistic. I have to admit, I'm disappointed. She doesn't love the things I love any more than I love all the things she does. I romanticized marriage.

"I talked with Pastor Stephens this morning. He helped me look at my situation more practically. He shared the Serenity Prayer. It's funny. I always thought it was for alcoholics. Yet here I am with it hanging from my rearview mirror. I highly recommend it." Jackson took a card from his wallet and passed it to Rachel.

"Hmmm." She read the card.

"God grant me the serenity to accept the things I cannot change.

The courage to change the things I can.

And the wisdom to know the difference."

"Wow! Seems I need it just the same."

"I love you, Rach."

"I love you too, Jackson."

The friends looked into each other's eyes and shared a smile. This was the way between them.

Chapter Fifteen

───── ≈ ─────

The late edition of the evening news ended. Rachel sat for a few moments in the quietness. She checked the time on her phone once. Then twice. "I just can't sit here anymore!" She headed outside and began pacing the driveway. John was expected any minute. Rachel wouldn't trade John and Jackson's annual trip to Peru for anything in the world. But ten days was about as long as she could handle being apart. Twenty-three years of trips had not changed that. The last leg from Atlanta seemed to take forever.

Rachel breathed a sigh of relief when the headlights turned toward the house. John pulled his truck into his usual spot in the carport with a smile on his face. He didn't turn off the ignition before stepping out and reaching for Rachel. She wholeheartedly submitted to his embrace. "Thank you, Lord, for getting my man home safely!"

She loved her familiar place in John's arms. He lifted Rachel's chin and delivered a soft kiss. Then another. "I've missed you so much. Day ten always does me in. There's no place like home!"

Rachel emptied John's duffle and sorted the dirty laundry while he checked in with Jackson. "I'm home. Apologize to Anastasia for the late call. Just following your orders." The two chatted briefly. "Tuesday at 7 a.m. As usual, we'll drive up tomorrow night. We'll give you a call after we meet with the doctor. Prayers please."

John headed off to the shower. As he got ready for bed, Rachel observed his movements. Covertly, as always. His stature seemed normal. Motor skills the same as prior to his trip. That was good news. But his use of painkillers had increased. In two days, Birmingham.

The University Hospital basement was full this morning. MRIs around the clock. Once John was taken back, Rachel sat among other loved ones. Waiting and wondering. Praying. Asking God to hold John…and to continue to hold her together.

As their routine dictated, a visit to the coffee shop was in order. A two-hour interim allowed for a few cups just blocks from the doctor's office. Rush-hour traffic was in full swing. From their patio table, a steady roar.

They sat quietly, sipping. A bird flitted around the table and then landed in between the couple. Rachel spoke to the delicate creature like a child, assuming crumbs were his purpose. There were none. The tiny visitor shifted his gaze back and forth between the two. As if they were known to him. He waited, giving each person time to take in the beauty he displayed. After a short delay, he departed.

"Was that a sparrow?" John nodded as he looked into the sky. "It sure was." They looked at the nearby trees. The parking deck across the street. Again to the sky. There were no birds today. None to be found. Only the lone sparrow that visited them while they waited. John and Rachel smiled and looked heavenward. Certainly, their little friend came to deliver a message from on high. "Isn't God good! His eye is on the sparrow, and I know he cares for me." John spoke with assurance.

The drive-through saw many patrons during the Averys' break. Though few entered the establishment. An elderly gentleman exited the shop with coffee in hand. He approached John and Rachel, who were the only customers on the patio. "Do you folks mind if I sit with you for a while?" In John Avery fashion, he stood and greeted the stranger with a handshake. "Be our guest, sir."

The voice of the visitor was soothing. Like a grandfather. "Thank you! Call me Archie." Archie was talkative. He questioned the Averys about their lives. The three talked about farming. Family. Children. Grandchildren. About the good old days. There were no questions presented about this particular day or their reason for being near the hospital.

Though a stranger, Archie seemed like an old friend. The time passed quickly. There had been no opportunity to circle back to the *what-ifs* that were common at this stage of the UH morning. John and Rachel were thankful for a pleasant distraction.

"I'm going to go now." John and Rachel both stood along with Archie. "It was nice sitting with you folks. You have to get to your appointment." Archie took Rachel's hands in his. She was uncomfortable with the initial touch of the stranger but submitted to a peace that came almost instantly. He looked intently into her eyes. "You're going to be alright, Miss."

Archie gave John a firm nod while lifting his suede Stetson. Then he moved toward the street. John and Rachel shared a questioning look, then immediately turned back to offer final salutations. Archie was gone.

Dr. Fain was the best of the best. He had seen much worse than a non-progressive midbrain tumor. The neuro-oncology waiting room was proof. Observing the struggles of patients to speak and to walk made John grateful that a checkup was their only purpose there. That confirmation of no change would come. That their lives would remain intact.

Nevertheless, John couldn't imagine the journey that brought each family to this place. A brief imagination was all his mind would allow. All his heart could handle. The two were called back almost immediately. The wait from there would be long.

For over four years, John and Rachel traveled three hours one way to meet with the experts. Today, they were optimistic. "I think Dr. Fain will ask us to come back in two years instead of one. Since there has been no change, as he told us from the beginning, the tumor could have been there my whole life. In the absence of brain scans from my childhood for comparisons, they have no way of knowing." Rachel contemplated John's evaluation. "Actually, I think you're going to be dismissed. If I'm right, you're buying lunch!" Spirits were high on this day. They were hopeful. Almost relieved by the prospects.

Dr. Fain was brilliant. He hosted physicians from around the globe to observe his practice. To learn from him. He was straightforward, sometimes abrasive. Though Rachel didn't appreciate his manner toward her husband's plight, she was aware he had seen brain disease take lives in horrific fashion. A soft heart's survival wasn't conducive on this battlefield.

Dr. Fain entered the room hastily with his foreign entourage. He sat before John and delivered the news. "Mr. Avery, the tumor has begun to grow!" John and Rachel were frozen in disbelief. Without moving his gaze from the doctor, John reached for Rachel's hand.

The words delivered that day changed everything. A follow-up scan confirmed continued growth in a short period of time. "The tumor is inoperable! It's growing in a most intricate place in the midbrain. Irreparable damage to your basic life functions would result if we trespassed there. It's a place we just can't go. We're not sure of the makeup of the tumor since we can't biopsy it. But we need to address the growth. We will proceed with targeted radiation here at UH. I am referring you to an excellent radiation neuro-oncologist. He also leads our brain tumor research. Dr. Britt."

Rachel began to research. It was her way. Medical journals became regular reading. She often read while John was sleeping. She never wanted to foster fear or doubt in him. Though she battled her own.

The prognosis was grim. Five years from diagnosis. John had already lived through more than four of those. Regardless of the science, the testing, and the research, faith had to stand at the forefront. Otherwise, the Averys couldn't stand at all. God was still their sustainer, their healer, and their source of all things. Above all, He was sovereign. Whatever came to them, no matter the degree of difficulty or struggle, they knew it couldn't come but through Him.

John moved into a sponsored apartment near the hospital during the period of daily radiation treatments. He was hours from home...from his Rachel. Red Mountain Grace brought hope and comfort to him as he struggled to think beyond each sunrise. The apartment was a blessing from those who answered the call to be doers of God's word.

Rachel had to keep working...in New Berry. She completed her degree and began teaching after Beth was born. The family's health insurance was maintained through her employer. Bills quickly piled up. Every person who touched John or his case required payment.

John looked forward to Thursdays when Rachel would travel to Birmingham to accompany him to meetings with specialists and to spend precious moments together. Six weeks seemed like six months. But the radiation ended. John had received the maximum dosage. The custom mask that held John's head securely to the treatment table horrified Rachel. She couldn't dispose of it fast enough.

"Radiation kills cancer. Radiation also causes cancer. Though we have confidence that the tumor will respond to treatment, it is possible that another tumor will eventually grow." John and Rachel were disappointed but thankful for Dr. Britt's honest projections. "The radiation can continue to work for up to eighteen months. We will check for improvement every eight weeks."

The two-month wait was grueling. When the day finally came, the results were disappointing. There was minimal change in the tumor. Other changes, however, were coming faster than they knew.

Before the sun set on the day, John was hospitalized. A neurosurgeon stood at his bedside. "Hydrocephalus! You're at an emergency level. The tumor, along with swelling from radiation treatments, has caused blockage of the cerebrospinal fluid. This is creating a great deal of intercranial pressure. I'm sure your headache has become unbearable." John nodded. He never complained, so even Rachel was unaware of the severity.

"The pressure has to be relieved or there will be damage to the brain. I need to make a cut in the ventricle floor, allowing the fluid to divert. In layman's terms, it's like a detour. This will reduce pressure and pain. I'll touch base with you in a few minutes, and we will start prepping."

Rachel could see the apprehension in John's eyes. "We just came for a doctor's appointment, and now I'm having brain surgery. Pray for me. Please pray for me now." Rachel leaned over, holding John in her arms.

"Heavenly Father, you have always been faithful. Always! We trust you. We give this surgery to you. Hold John in the palm of your hand. Blanket him with your peace. Guide the surgeon. Guide every medical professional who touches him. Show yourself strong and mighty on his behalf! On our behalf! In Jesus name!"

The surgeon stuck her head back in the room.

"Are your kids here yet?"

"We need thirty more minutes," Rachel estimated.

"You've got it. As soon as they are here, we're going in."

Within the hour, John was prepped and ready for surgery. He lay in a holding pattern. The unknown before him. *Jesus, walk me through this.* He was wheeled into the operating room. The bright lights forced his eyes shut. *Jesus, hold Rachel, Jacq, Faith, Beth, four, three, two....*

Everyone was in place in the waiting room. An emotional fog settled. Jackson and Uncle Jimmy held Faith and Beth close. Rachel sat in a stupor. Anxiety and trust milled about within her in equal parts. Tears emerged and receded like ocean waves. Jacq stayed close to her mother. Her prayers were constant. All waited for their beloved husband, Daddy, Poppy, and friend. Who were they really without him?

The phone call came for Rachel. "The surgery went well. The fluid is moving. The pressure is reducing. His pain level should respond accordingly." Rachel breathed a sigh of relief. "While I was in, I attempted to retrieve a biopsy. I needed a small sample to identify the grade and biomarkers. That didn't happen. I couldn't risk causing irreparable damage. The most pressing problem has been addressed."

"Thank you, doctor! Thank you from the bottom of my heart!"

"Mr. Avery will be in recovery for a while, then we will transfer him to the NICU. Go ahead and head that way. When he's settled, a nurse will take you to him. God bless you all!"

The family took the long trek to the Neurosciences Intensive Care Unit. The University Hospital was enormous, the square footage unmatched, and the halls a maze. They arrived exhausted. Hungry. Disoriented. Yet no one complained. How could they?

Rachel entered the enormous waiting room and scanned. She was in disbelief. At this late hour, it looked like a shanty town. There was a makeshift tent in the corner, with a few sleeping bags dispersed against a wall. Loved ones marked their territories with chairs. Some squared off areas like tiny rooms with their belongings. Rachel's heart broke.

The crew found seating and huddled together. The girls tried to nap. Rachel took out her phone. As she gained Wi-Fi access, messages loaded in record time. Over a hundred messages. Prayers and encouragement came from family, church, school, and the community. And one message from Jackson, who was four seats away from her.

How are you holding up? She peered over her sleeping daughters to see Jackson and Uncle Jimmy looking her way. Concern enveloped their faces. She returned to her phone screen, selecting a *thumbs up* and a *heart*, and then pressed send. What would their family ever do without the two of them? She hoped they never had to find out.

Messages from Rachel's accountability group brought beautiful notes of hope and encouragement. For twenty-five years, Rachel and these women shared their walks of life. They raised their children together. Walked out triumphs and tragedies. *The Crazies*, they called themselves. Comrades who would do whatever it took to get a hurting friend to the feet of Jesus. The second chapter of the book of Mark was their foundation.

Today, her *Crazies*, along with an entire community, symbolically lowered the Averys to Jesus in prayer. In this lowest valley, gratitude flooded Rachel's heart. How beautifully God provided. How blessed to be surrounded by so much love.

"You folks new here?" an older lady crouched in the corner asked without looking up from her book. "Yes, ma'am. My husband had surgery this evening. Hydrocephalus. He has a brain tumor."

"I'm sorry about that. Keep your belongings close. We've had vagrants wander in during the night to help themselves." Rachel affirmed with a nod, not wanting to hear any more bad news.

"Some of us have been here a while. As you can see. My son's back there. His brain surgery came after head trauma from a car accident. On my birthday. I sent him to the store to get napkins. He never made it home." Rachel's name was called as a nurse stepped out from a long hallway.

She arose without hesitation to follow, then turned back. "I'm sorry about your son." The lady lowered her book and gave an accepting smile. "You'll be able to handle much more than you ever thought possible. I promise." Rachel's chin began to quiver, but she could produce no words.

As soon as they entered the hallway, the nurse began giving instructions. "You will be able to stay with Mr. Avery back here. There's a reclining chair. I'll sneak you a blanket. We will run you out from 6 a.m. to 8 a.m. Same in the evening. Let's us get some work done with no distractions. You'll need that time away. Even if it's just for a cup of coffee. You don't realize now, but you will.

"Only two visitors at a time. One for overnight. I'm Mr. Avery's dedicated nurse tonight. He'll require a lot of care while here. I only have one other patient. Any questions? Anything I can get for you?" She waited. "Mrs. Avery?"

Rachel was overwhelmed. She heard the words. Her tired mind was simply processing more slowly than normal. "No questions." They moved past several glass enclosures, each with its own version of a crumpled, bedridden figure. They paused in front of number fourteen.

There was John Avery. A very different vision from the man she had last seen. Wires, tubes, machines and drip bags. Her tears came quietly. Strength wasn't an option in this moment. There was no use.

The nurse rested her hand on John's shoulder. "Mr. Avery, your wife is here." No response came. She cast Rachel a reassuring smile and then left them. Rachel lowered herself to the edge of the bed, cupping John's cold hands between hers. Tears dropped like rain on the white sheet that outlined his body.

Just months earlier, they had watched this dreaded disease from a distance. Almost through a veil. John and Rachel had rested in the bliss that ignorance of it provided. Now, they had fallen headlong into the throes of brain cancer. Seventeen staples lined John's scalp. An exterior manifestation of the thief that lay within. Proof that it was all real. Too real. They were no longer the exception. They were the rule.

Chapter Sixteen

"Meet me at the old homeplace in fifteen minutes," Rachel's text read. Jackson slipped his boots on. He left a brief note on the kitchen table for Uncle Jimmy, then headed that way. He couldn't help but wonder what was up. John was only released from UH the day before.

The weeklong hospital stay seemed longer. There was no tired like hospital tired. John was in a deep sleep for many hours each day after the surgery. Rachel rarely slept. The Unit was alive day and night as professionals moved about completing their tasks. Rachel stayed near. Each time John awoke, she wanted her face to be the first he saw.

Rachel wanted to be strong for John. For everyone. She tried to be brave. Though at times faking it was all she could muster. Times when fear set in or when a weariness settled on her whole being. Though she was a mess, she refused to let weakness triumph. "This is a marathon, not a sprint." So she had been told.

Rachel's mind often revisited Mr. and Mrs. Avery's plight decades earlier. How Mrs. Avery's strength was always at the forefront. She wondered about the details now. How did she survive the emotional strain from day to day?

Did she sleep at night? How did she put one foot in front of the other? The one thing she knew for sure was that Mrs. Avery stood beside her husband until his last breath. Rachel admired her for her example.

Jackson pulled up to the abandoned structure. Rachel's car was near the road. She was not. He stepped out of his pickup, scanning the surrounding countryside. The small parcel of land arose at a slight elevation. From it, farm views were stunning on all sides.

East to west, it captured clear views of sunrises and sunsets beyond the distant tree lines. To the north, cattle dotted the rolling hills. Sloping pastures to the south were home to sheep and horses grazing the browning grasses. And the house. The house that was once a showstopper sat silent in the midst of it all.

Just months ago, the gardens had a burst of summer life that launched growth well beyond their borders. Year after year. More and more. The departure of autumn slightly subdued the overgrowth of running roses and wisteria. Then all went into a deep sleep. Once beautiful, now messy and unkempt. All lay dormant. Forgotten for half a century.

Jackson made his way around the shaded side of the house through fallen pecans and accumulated leaves. He meandered through the trail of bud-covered camellias, awaiting a chill that would open their delightful winter blooms of pink, red, and white.

Rachel stood at the far back of the lot, where the St. Augustine blades met the farrowed field. She stared over the back forty. The afternoon sun cast a shadow of her figure before her. Her stance was like a rag doll's. Her shoulders slumped. Arms drooped. "Rachel?" Jackson stood back, not wanting to startle her. There was no movement. No response.

Concern swept over him. He moved toward her. "Rachel?" His projection was stronger. She lifted a few fingers from her side in a directive. He stopped. Her head dropped.

Jackson awaited her response. Rachel's fingers folded in toward her palms in labored movements, the left and right hands forming fists simultaneously. With every moment, her body became tense and rigid. She raised her fists from her side into the still air, shaking them in a display of angered helplessness.

Rachel's entire body reacted. The fear and frustration that had built since the shocking revelation of John's prognosis erupted in a raging scream. The entire landscape shuttered as the response emerged from her body.

Jackson was startled. Birds fluttered from the grasses. Rachel regurgitated the emotion she held. All she had seen, heard, and felt burst forth. Her body folded forward in a slow motion as the evidence of the emotion left her. As the outburst, in increments, cleansed her.

As the scream subsided, tears surged. Deep, agonizing tears. Tears that dripped of pain and fear…and love. Rachel dropped to her knees. Jackson rushed forward, sliding in close behind her to catch her. She slumped further to the ground. Jackson embraced her shoulders and leaned her body back toward him. "I've got you, Rachel."

The sobs turned to quiet tears that washed over Rachel's being. Over her heart and her mind. Her hopes and dreams. The flow couldn't be stopped. It had to run its course.

Rachel remained pressed against Jackson until the heaviness of the emotion had been expelled. She was still. So spent that her entire body lay limp. Almost lifeless. Her eyes closed.

Jackson cradled Rachel like a baby. He pulled a handkerchief from his back pocket. With great care, he wiped the wet strands away from her forehead and the evidence of her tears from her face. He stared at her as she rested against him. Her look was pure and gentle.

Rachel wore her strength—her assurance—like a soldier's armor. In this moment, however, he saw beyond that. He saw her vulnerability. What she never wanted others to discover. He saw a love so deep for his best friend that it enveloped her whole being. *Oh, to be loved like this!*

Rachel was depleted…physically and emotionally. She submitted to sleep as Jackson rocked her in his arms. Gentle quivers sounded with each breath. A comforting shade moved over the two as the battered gable sheltered the afternoon sun.

Several minutes passed, and Rachel opened her eyes. She looked up at Jackson, who was looking down at her. He smiled his quirky smile. "Hello. You feeling any better?" It took a few moments for Rachel's mind to make sense of where she was and what had just transpired. She sat up.

"I am so sorry! That was all unexpected!" Jackson laughed. "Yeah, I can relate." Rachel's gaze snapped back at him, responding to his sarcasm. She gave him a sassy push. He offered his handkerchief, which she gladly received. "Last year's birthday present. I chose this font for the monogram very carefully." With expected etiquette, she turned away, tending to her stuffy nose. She turned back to her friend with a soft grin. "You want this back?" He twisted his face. "Nah. I think I'll let you keep it. I have nine more just like it." They both laughed as Jackson helped Rachel up from the grass.

"What's on your mind, Rachel? Besides the obvious." She turned to face the house, whose back screen door was hanging by one hinge. "This is what's on my mind!" I want to move John in here. He and I should have done it years ago. It was just easier to stay at The Manor. Now, it's time!" Jackson looked at Rachel and then at the house. Then Rachel. "Hmmm."

"Yes, I know it's rough! To the naked eye. I see its potential. I know you do too."

"Three-inch pine floors. They are in great shape. The walls are one by six pine. Most rooms still have the original wall covering used when the house was built in 1920. I peeled some back. The wood looks almost brand new.

The crawl space looks good. The sills are in great shape. It will need a new roof. Has to be rewired and replumbed. It needs HVAC. That's just to start."

"I'd like to keep the old windows for now—" Jackson interrupted. "Sounds like you have it all figured out." Rachel peered at him. "No. I'm going to need lots of help, but I wasn't born yesterday!" She stopped short, cupping her hands over her face.

"Rachel?" Jackson poised himself for another episode.

"Jackson, it's hard to explain. I feel the need to make plans. To see the reality that is before us. To accept what is happening in John's body. To make what could be his last days, his last holiday, the best it possibly could be. To create memories that our daughters and grandchildren can carry for their lifetimes. At the same time, I can't release the hope that comes with our faith. Our belief that God is still in the business of healing.

"I'm on a tightrope, balancing what is before me. I want to move forward and make this house a home. The Avery home. Not a place for John to die. A place for him to live. I have to move forward for his life. We are going to do this believing that he will spend the next forty years here. Beyond that belief, my heart can't go. Not yet.

"Faith is not denial. I see what is happening. It's real. But I must live in the hope that my God can and will turn it all around in the blink of an eye. He has always worked everything together for good. Sometimes in ways we certainly didn't understand. But he has proven Himself through Romans 8:28 time and time again. Even when we couldn't see the big picture, He was working. God has been faithful!

"This house will be a place of rest, renewal, and restoration. Now and for all the generations to come. We'll call her The Renaissance House."

Jackson pursed his lips. Tears welled in his eyes. He swallowed hard and then turned away from Rachel. "Hmmm. Look who's crying now!" He laughed and reached back around, roughing up Rachel's hair.

"JACKSON!!"

"I'm in. When do you want to start?"

"ASAP! The money's in the bank. I've been saving since we got married. Living in The Manor made that possible."

Rachel and Jackson spent a few hours going through the house and making lists.

"I want him in here by Christmas." She looked up to Jackson for reassurance.

"Christmas it is!"

"Great! Just one more thing to ensure my cart isn't before the horse." She turned toward the door, then back to Jackson. "Hey. Thank you. For everything."

Jackson offered a simple smile and a nod.

Rachel leaned in, kissing John on the forehead. "You want to go for a ride while the girls cook dinner?" John was gaining a degree of mobility with every day beyond his surgery. Though still weak and shaky. "Yes. Please get me out of this house. A ride in the country would be great." Rachel helped John out of the house and into the car. "I guess you're my chauffeur now?" She climbed into the driver's seat. "Yep. Your life is in my hands."

Rachel had never been the driver. If gender roles existed between them, this was one of them. John drove when the two were together. She liked it that way. And trash. He took out the trash. Everything else was equal between them. Almost.

She stopped in the front yard of their old homeplace, where they had dreamed many times before. The late afternoon sun reflected a golden glow off the tall windows that adorned the front of the home. It gave a welcoming appearance, as if lights were on inside. A welcome that nature provided.

It was a warm day for the first of November. Alabama's weather was that way. Seasons were never distinct. They milled in and out among one another. Sharing days. Yet rarely standing alone. Now, a chill was building in the breeze. Rachel pulled a blanket from the backseat and spread it over John's lap.

"Don't you think it's time for us to come home?" John turned to Rachel, wondering what was coming next. "I've prayed for a while about this. I have peace that now is the time. But I won't make a move unless I know we are one in this decision." John looked back at the house, then returned his eyes to hers with a confident smile. "I agree. It's time. I know much of the responsibility will fall to you. I trust you. I will do as much as I can for as long as I can."

Rachel was thankful for unity. The two sat until the darkness sent them away.

Jackson, Uncle Jimmy and Rachel rallied at the Averys' after church. The project had the green light. Jackson started. "I will be in Atlanta during the week and in New Berry on the weekends. Anastasia understands that this timetable is critical. If we get pushed toward the end, I will take leave from the hospital. Uncle Jimmy, I realize you need to work in John's place in the hardware store. Can we order our materials and supplies through you?" Uncle Jimmy straightened up. "Absolutely!"

Jackson turned to Rachel. "Uncle Jimmy and I have no doubt that your brother Simon is the best of the best, and we have asked him to oversee the project. He will bring in his crew. He's on board and so happy to do something to show his love for you and your family."

Buster's son, Simon, was overseas with the Navy when Rachel arrived on the scene. She never knew him. It wasn't until Buster's funeral that they began to build a relationship and form a bond. For a little misplaced girl who strove to belong, God had surrounded her with more love than her heart could even hold.

As word spread about John and The Renaissance House, volunteers showed up in record numbers. Community, church members, friends. *The*

Crazies were ever present, working, praying, and cooking. Pate and Deborah arrived with tools in hand. Ann and Aunt Ella volunteered.

Even Anastasia made an appearance.

All of Rachel's siblings were present, along with her work family. Everyone pitched in as directed by Simon. Thomas Stein, as kind as ever, volunteered to assist the driveway crew. In the midst of struggle, Rachel's world was coming full circle.

Rachel took an early retirement. Caring for John was the most important work she could do. His body grew weaker. More frail. Muscle wasting, they called it. John would have given anything to work alongside Rachel and his friends on their farmhouse. On his few good days, he sat near windows, scraping paint on their lower portions. With rooms surrounded by windows, John's contribution was substantial. He needed to feel useful.

When move-in day came, everyone felt a sense of accomplishment.

What a blessed day it was for John and Rachel Avery. Christmas Day with all the children and grandchildren under one roof. All under the roof of their new home. The home of which they had dreamed was now their reality.

John's physical struggle was taxing. His leather recliner served as his roost as his precious family moved about in the excitement of the day. Hearing *Poppy* from the littles was all the present he needed. All he really wanted. He watched their comings and goings under the powerful effects of rounds of morphine. Each step on the newly stained hardwoods seemed magnified by his prescribed steroids.

John took it all in and smiled at the commotion. The young men hung his gift from Rachel. The daughters directed the task. An old oxen yoke was mounted. *Come unto me!* it called out.

The grandchildren danced on the handmade coffee table as they sang along to Rudolph the Red-Nosed Reindeer. Rounds of sweet potato pie were consumed. Hot chocolate sipped in ceramic snowman mugs. Miniature marshmallows in excess pilfered by tiny hands.

Rachel entered the gathering room from the kitchen. A lump caught in her throat as the scene interrupted her busyness. She paused, taking in the emotions of this room so full of all she loved. She committed every detail to memory. Every interaction. The sights. The sounds. The smells. Her heart recorded it all.

John nodded for Rachel. With labored speech, he directed his wife. "Put on your coat. Your gift from me…is in the…front yard. I guess it's from Jackson…and me." He smiled. It was good to see John smile. "I was the… brains. He was the…brawn. Wrap up…and spend a few quiet moments… out under the old Eliot…in the front yard." Rachel returned a questioning look. For a moment, she was like a child. The excitement of Christmas Day. A surprise. As she left the house, Rachel looked back to see the family gathering at the windows. All except John.

She walked toward the aged pecan tree that sat in the far corner of the front yard. As she passed the stately bottle brush that surprisingly still carried its red blooms, she saw it. Her swing. Jackson moved it from The Manor. He placed its new frame perfectly. Three-gallon gardenias were planted about. The old-fashioned variety she loved so much. Rachel was thrilled. What could the two have given her that she would love more?

She sat, leaning into its familiar motion. It was like an old friend. It embraced her as it had so many times. Times when life was good. Times when it was not. It heard the triumphs and the struggles they had all lived. Together. Rachel lingered in the quietness, contemplating. What did this dear friend still have to learn from her—from them—in the new season that awaited them?

Rachel's friend, Sarah, arrived with her husband, Ben, to convey a priceless Christmas gift for the Averys. *The Crazies* served one another in just that way.

The Averys, from oldest to youngest, put on their layers and gathered on the chilled front porch. John held tightly to Rachel and Jacq on the top step. His position was front and center. Rachel took her place next to John, the man with whom she had shared life and love and who was the revelation of the promise God made to her as a child, arm in arm.

Sarah organized each family member. Rich and Jacq sat on the lower steps. Stella snuggled into her mother's lap. Faith stood behind her father and leaned back into Zane with Baby Isabel in her arms. Hope sat on the porch railing with her parents, Beth and Dan, on either side.

The family was in position. The old house had opened its arms and welcomed them. It had come alive for what remained. It found a family. A family found a home.

"Ready? Everyone smile! Say, "Merry Christmas!""

Chapter Seventeen

Rachel managed John's frail body into her van. The effort exhausted both. She slid his walking cane in by the automatic door. This was not just any cane. It was John's father's. Mr. Avery carried it close during his illness decades earlier. It wasn't the safest walking aid. It served as more of an emotional support than physical. Like a security blanket connecting John to his past. Security. And comfort.

John lay on a makeshift bed created over the stowed seats in Rachel's van, which they kept though their children protested. They saw no need for it. A car would be more appropriate since she and John were empty-nesters. They teased about her *mom* van. Until now. The entire rear was converted. With the seats stowed, she could haul half a house, or so she bragged. It had carried many antiques to and from their home.

Now, Rachel transported her most precious cargo. She ensured that John was as comfortable as possible. Blankets were piled on a soft, cushioned pallet. From the driver's seat, she could monitor her patient. When John's head lowered to the pillow and Rachel tucked a blanket snuggly around his weakened frame, he fell fast asleep. His new normal.

A tag hung from the rearview mirror reflected John's current physical status. *Handicapped,* it read. Rachel fought it in her mind. It felt like giving up. As if their faith were impotent. Now, every decision was for John's comfort.

Rachel placed loaded suitcases at the back of the van, near the hatch. They held enough clothes to last for weeks. She couldn't decide what to pack, so she didn't decide. She packed a little of everything. Rachel's mind was tired. She was in survival mode. Her ability to organize and plan was waning.

John and Rachel needed a break from the place of their struggle. Even if for only a few days. There was only one place that could soothe their hearts right now. Perry and Leigh's home. The two had taken up residence at Perry's old family homestead, which had been passed down through the generations. The Hastings called Kentucky their home for two decades. The Averys traveled there annually. They were family.

New Year's Eve at five degrees was perfect. The glow of the post-Christmas tree. A continuous supply of wood in the fireplace. Perry's standing rib roast with his signature horseradish sauce paired with Leigh's roasted vegetables and homemade yeast rolls. Her lemon meringue pie for dessert. Delicious food, friendship and laughter. And the reminders woven into their conversations of their God, who had always been faithful.

There was no fireworks display deep in this country setting on the eve of the new year. But the stars...the stars put on the best show they had ever seen. For as far as their eyes could see, God displayed his splendor of twinkling lights. His presence was evident in his handiwork. In the midst of their crisis, the Averys relished every moment.

Leigh and Rachel were up early on New Year's Day. Hot coffee by the fire was delightful. Through the north window, cardinals rushed the feeder among dangling icicles. Frost created a winter wonderland among the trees, the meadow, the barn, the smokehouse and over the adjoining mountains. In the distance, a low fog hovered over the curves of the Cumberland meandering through the foothills. The sights of the undisturbed winter morn offered tranquility.

"I'm glad you drove up. I know it wasn't easy getting here. We're glad to have these moments with the two of you." Rachel stared into the flames. "This was where we wanted to be. Where we needed to be." She looked at Leigh. "Thank you for always opening your door and your hearts to us."

Perry strolled into the kitchen, offering greetings and reaching for the beans and grinder for his morning brew. He began pulling ingredients for his traditional biscuits. Leigh and Rachel joined him at the island. "Rachel, we see how John is doing physically. How is he emotionally? How is he coping?" Perry paused from breakfast preparation, awaiting Rachel's response. "That's certainly a loaded question. It's more complex than I ever imagined.

"The loss of his independence has been most difficult for him. When he had to take leave from his job, he struggled, knowing Uncle Jimmy was carrying the load. It ate at him. Being dependable. Being responsible. Taking care of others. It has never been just what he did. It has always been who he is.

"I had to hide his truck keys. Driving hasn't been an option for a while. Not even around the farm. Vision loss, hallucinations and confusion took that from him. When I told him he couldn't drive, he looked like a little child being reprimanded.

"When I could no longer leave him alone at home, he was pitiful. He keeps apologizing. He thinks he's a burden. I wish I could do more. I wish I could fix this. Helplessness has not been a good place to be...for either of us.

"He has no doubt our girls and grandchildren will be well taken care of. Their husbands are amazing. We've been assured since the beginning that God ordained each union. That brings great peace. Leaving me is what's weighing heavy on his mind. He's so worried about how I will make it without him. That's just like him to think of me before himself. That's who he is!"

"Rachel, how are you holding up?"

"I miss him. John is disappearing before my eyes. This disease is taking him from me bit by bit. I'm weary, but I want to do right by him for the rest of our days. Whether that is one day or a thousand, I'm determined to be there for him the way he has always been there for me.

"I thought I was a strong woman. Through this, I've learned I was strong because John's love built a firm foundation. He's always been there for me. Making a way. Loving. Supporting. Cheering me on. I have lived a blessed life with that man lying in there. I don't think I fully grasped it until now."

The University Hospital appointment was more difficult this round. Walking was not an option for John. Instability was a liability. Personal wheelchair transports within the facility were a phone call away.

Today's schedule was predictable. An MRI, then an appointment with both doctors. The coffee shop visit was eliminated. Even the short stent for the break was more than John and Rachel could handle. The two would remain in Dr. Fain's waiting room. Waiting and wondering about the outcome.

Rachel looked out across the room as John napped. She knew the patients who sat here for the first time. She could see their fear. Their anxiety. As they took in the surroundings. As they prayed that what they saw would never come to them. Some were oblivious. As she and John had once been. *Lord, hold them in your arms. Please hold them.*

The prior month had seen a great decline for John. In all areas. Mental capacity. Vision. Mobility. Everything was a struggle. Pain was ever-present. Increased sleep had become a blessing.

"John Avery!" A call came across the crowded room. Rachel gathered their belongings and maneuvered the reclined wheelchair toward the awaiting nurse. "Dr. Fain asked us to call you back as soon as you arrived. Let's get vitals, then I'll put you in a room."

They waited in complete stillness. The tiny room was their temporary solace. Neither speculated. There was no small talk. The outside world moved about at hyperspeed. All sounded normal beyond the door. Lunch orders were taken. Conversations and laughter echoed through the hallway. The

Averys remained in silence. John lay on the exam table, drifting in and out of sleep. Lucidity was not his companion on this day.

Dr. Fain entered with no cheerful greeting. No observer introductions. He was accompanied by their friend, Dr. Britt. Rachel held her breath. "The news is not good. Today, your images show multiple tumors in the brain. All the symptoms you shared since your last MRI line up with what we see today. There's nothing more we can do. We're very sorry."

For a moment, there was complete silence.

Rachel looked at John, whose eyes remained closed. *Did he understand? Had he even heard the report?* With no movement and his eyes still closed, he spoke. "What will…the end be?"

Dr. Britt arose, placing his hand on John's shoulder. He had been their guardian angel, walking them through an impossible journey with respect and compassion. Though brilliant in his profession, the way in which he cared for the Averys was the medicine that saved them. Their gratitude would be eternal.

Dr. Fain turned back to the computer images. "Two months at the most. I wish I could assure you of more. All symptoms will intensify. Hallucinations. Confusion. Pain. Eventually, you will go into a deep sleep. Heart rate will slow. Then respirations…until all ceases."

The trip back to New Berry was quiet. John slept. Rachel tried to push the prognosis out of her mind. It was Dr. Britt's final words that lingered in her thoughts.

"I wanted you both to know how absolutely impressed I have been with the way you have cared for one another over these years. The way you shared the burden. As you yoked yourselves for this challenge, you mastered it admirably." Rachel held his words close to her heart. Again, God held her tears.

Rachel wasn't sure how they got home. She couldn't remember much of the drive. The shock had dropped a veil. A fog. She thanked God when they were again at The Renaissance House and John was tucked in. "I thought... we could beat this. I thought together...we could beat this." She delivered a kiss to John's forehead and a gentle hug. "Shhh. Rest now. I love you." She, too, believed they would overcome. The ravages of the evolving glioblastoma had no mercy.

Rachel began her chores immediately. She had to stay on top of the work, or it would overtake her. Clothes needed to be washed, dried, and put away. The kitchen needed to be cleaned. Bills needed to be paid. Medicines needed to be dispensed in weekly containers. All before her head hit the pillow. Staying organized helped Rachel keep her sanity. Chores could be controlled in her world, which seemed completely out of control.

The following day, the Avery daughters would be in from their respective states. They would lift the load. Uncle Jimmy would drop by, as he regularly did, to see if any help was needed. Even though he was working double time. And Jackson. Rachel had not heard from Jackson since she sent word earlier in the morning about the report John received. His silence was unusual. Disturbing.

Kate and Susan came to the back door with casseroles in hand. What a blessing to be cared for by her *Crazies*. A few minutes of girl talk and prayer were priceless. Rachel coveted every second of the visit and was thrilled to have a hot meal delivered to their door.

When the ladies had gone, Rachel lingered on the back porch, taking in the beauty of the evening sky. The moon cast a glow over the back field. She glanced over at John's favorite porch chair. It had been empty for far too long.

Rachel returned to the kitchen to prepare John's dinner tray. The aroma was tantalizing. *Thank you, Lord, for good friends!* Rachel served John's plate and reached for a fork. As she moved, she heard a flutter above her head. A tiny robin had perched on the light fixture. The visitor flew in undetected as

Rachel talked with her friends. She had no idea how she would remove the trespasser without John's help.

There were antiques and artifacts throughout the room. Above the cabinets. On the refrigerator. Displayed on shelving and arranged on the ten-foot windowsill. The bird's movements could cause a disaster in any direction. She turned off the kitchen light. The whole house was dark. The only light was cast on the porch at the back door. She hoped the bird would fly in that direction.

Rachel heard movement, followed by a small crash. She could barely see a flutter on the windowsill. Moving to the window, she picked up the chirping visitor, setting him free in the backyard.

Rachel returned to find the item that had been disturbed. She turned on the light, picking up a small frame that had fallen from the center of the sill into the sink. Her lip began to quiver. Of all that was displayed in Rachel's busy kitchen, the tiny bird knocked over only one item. As the realization hit Rachel, she dropped to her knees and wept. The bird had knocked over a framed scripture from 2 Chronicles 20:15, which read:

Be not afraid, nor dismayed.

For the battle is not yours, but God's.

Rachel sat on the floor, crying. Praying. Thanking God for seeing her. As John's health declined, Rachel wrung her hands. Had she prayed enough? Believed enough? Had she researched enough? Had any of her efforts been enough?

God knew the parts of Rachel deep down inside that no one saw. The parts that had been with her since the beginning. Her struggle to please. To work to earn love and approval. He knew she would see John's death as her failure. That she had failed him. Failed her children. Maybe even failed God.

In that one moment, Rachel was released from the burden of carrying responsibility in this battle. A battle that was never meant to be hers. He was speaking to her. Through a tiny being in His creation, He sent a message. *There was a God...and she was not Him.* Her God was indeed sovereign.

Rachel held her fingers under the faucet, ensuring the flow didn't exceed an appropriate temperature. As light broke the horizon, she rested the pan of warm water on the table at their bedside. Soap, razor, washcloth, and towel in hand.

John looked into Rachel's eyes. He watched her motions. Warm strokes with the cloth moved over his face and neck. She bathed him with great care and dried his skin in loving, soft movements. John closed his eyes, relishing Rachel's touch.

Rachel applied soap to John's stubbled face. She moved the razor along his cheeks and the curves of his chin. The strokes were careful. Even. Intentional. She patted his skin dry, then rubbed her fingers across the still-warm surface. Leaning in, she kissed his smooth cheeks, then his mouth. He welcomed her kiss.

"Stay...with me." Rachel slipped off her shoes and climbed under the covers. John reached for her. As he had done so many times before. She moved back into his embrace, resting against his body. Their familiar place. The two looked beyond their window at the views of Avery Farms. The scene was soothing. The land that held their memories.

"I love you more than you'll ever know." John's whisper drifted into Rachel's ear. She was thankful for his mind's clarity this morning. It was rare in these difficult days. She closed her eyes, settling deeper into his warmth.

Her heart began to melt through the tears that eased onto her pillow. John reached over, gathering Rachel's hair. He gently moved it from her neck and began to thread his fingers through her locks. "John, what am I going to do without you?"

His words were firm. Clear.

"You'll keep...going."

"Don't let this...stop you."

"You have to keep...going."

Chapter Eighteen

―――――≈―――――

Rachel snuggled into the warm sheets. Into the spot her body had wallowed over time. She reached out with her foot across their king-sized bed. Reaching for John. To touch him, as was her routine. Just the slightest touch would suffice. Her search returned nothing. She stretched out again. Still nothing. Only an emptiness void of warmth. A cold, empty place.

Rachel sat straight up in bed. Into the pitch-black night. As she stared into the void, her shoulders relaxed. *John's in the bathroom.* She returned to her pillow, listening for the door to open. For John's steps. For one sound. One movement. The silence was stifling. "John?" She waited. "John, are you there?" *Please, Lord, let him answer.* The realization settled on her soul. There was no response.

Rachel rolled over, placing her hand on John's side of the bed. The covers were undisturbed, his pillows still neatly displayed. A single tear slid down the side of her face to her ear. Surely she had dreamed it all, but it was her new reality. Days had come and gone that shifted her world on its axis. Days that brought an unknown trajectory from which she could never return.

There was a numbness that accompanied the initial shock of John's death. It held everything in a manageable place. Rachel discovered that grief didn't arrive immediately. It would arrive later and stay longer. Much longer.

Rachel sat alone with a cup of coffee. It was 3 a.m. The structure of her days was lost. They no longer made sense. Night became day. Day became night. She lingered in the silence as the hours passed.

The sun finally peaked over the tree line at the back of the field. Rachel stepped onto the porch, still groggy from only a few hours of sleep. Her eyes scanned the landscape. As the barn came into view, there it was. The trash can. It was Thursday morning. Thursday was trash day. She had forgotten again.

Tears erupted. That was John's job. But John was gone. She would never again hear the bumbling of the plastic wheels on the concrete as he walked the trash down the driveway. Never. Each lapse of memory accentuated the absence of the man who held her life together.

Rachel longed for nights on the back porch. Holding hands. Even if neither had anything of importance to say. Sitting down to dinner and sharing a prayer. Touching each other in the darkness as they drifted off to sleep. The little things that were not so little after all.

It was all the acts of kindness that said *I love you!* with no words. Waking her with morning coffee. Warming her car on chilly days. The hot bath he ran on nights when he knew just what she needed. A new tube of ChapStick for her purse. He showed his feelings in many little ways that added up to a precious love.

Now, in her aloneness, she couldn't even remember the trash. "John!" She pounded her fist against the French door as the frustration spilled out. "Why did you leave me here? I don't want to be here without you!"

Remorse for her outrage came instantly. "Oh Lord, I'm sorry. I just miss him so much!" She paused to catch her breath. "I wouldn't want John to endure even one more day of pain on this earth. But I don't know how to do life without him. Help me, please."

She gathered the trash and then rushed out to the green can that had become a constant source of mockery. Still in her pajamas and robe, she pulled it down the curved, sloping driveway to the road. The truck could be heard a few farms away in the distance. She made it. A small obstacle had been conquered. For today.

Thank you, Lord, for the little blessings. Rachel chuckled through her tears. As she strolled back to the house feeling relieved, she took in the beauty of the dawn: the dew sparkling in the grass, the pink-tinted sky, and the birds jabbering their morning messages.

Rachel squinted toward the sun, which was now well over the horizon. Casting its warmth over the farm. Through the rays, she glimpsed the fowl. His gentle movement held her gaze as it descended toward her. It was the hawk. Her hawk. It had become a symbol for Rachel. A symbol of hope and assurance through the years of hardship. It was the almost supernatural sight of the hawk that reminded Rachel that her God's eyes were always on her.

She recalled the first day the white hawk flew in front of her car. It was the day the tumor took center stage in their lives. Her friend made its presence known each day she drove to the hospital. On many days of struggle. And the day John left their world. As the family looked out over the terraces of the farm. God reminded. *I see you. I'm with you.*

Rachel knew God could use anything to speak to his children...and He did. The Father's eyes never left her. On this day, she was reminded of that assurance. Her chenille sleeve wiped away her sadness. She straightened herself, breathing in the confidence that accompanied His reminder. "Your mercies truly are new every morning." Rachel landed on the couch. Finally, sleep overtook her.

"Knock, knock! Rachel?" Uncle Jimmy arrived, popping his head in the back door. Biscuits in hand. "Rachel, are you up?" She stepped out of the gathering room. "Hi, Uncle Jimmy. Yes, I'm up. I always seem to be up. Day and night." He knew Rachel would skip meals. Whether she would eat or not, he made sure there was food in the house. "I have your breakfast. Let me warm that coffee up for you."

Rachel leaned back on the long, padded church pew stationed alongside the farmhouse table. She was too tired to protest this morning. She knew Uncle Jimmy just wanted to help. He missed John too. He was trying to navigate the loss just the same.

"Come sit with me. We'll have breakfast together." Uncle Jimmy was happy to comply. As she ate her biscuit, Rachel pulled back the corner of the tablecloth, exposing the aged wood beneath. John made the family table from the old corn crib door that once hung in the first barn built on Avery Farms. Four twelve-inch boards. Each eight feet long. Planks that reflected years of hard times. Everything that John's hands touched also touched Rachel's heart.

"I've never experienced anything that compares to losing John. Life alone looks so different than life together. I'm relearning how to do practically everything. Like having an arm tied behind my back and trying to carry on as normal. Every task reminds me of his absence, whether great or small. The whole world looks different. Feels different. The world IS different."

Uncle Jimmy looked on with no expression. "You know exactly what I'm going through, don't you?" He dropped his head and wiped a tear. Rachel had no desire to navigate this new life. She didn't choose grief. It chose her.

There was constant contact with the Crazies, the Hastings, the Scotts and Kaye. The church took good care of Rachel. She never lacked for company or food. Friends and family were in and out of the house. Over the days. Over the weeks. Less as the months passed.

Rachel had the opportunity to spend time with friends. Though she often declined. It was companionship for which her heart longed. Losing it meant turning in bed to share the simplest tidbit and finding no ears to hear. Needing to share a painful experience or a triumph and speaking into the void. Picking up the phone only to realize John would not be answering.

Reaching out to touch in the night and being unfulfilled.

John and Rachel were one. She had not determined how to live when part of her was gone. When she was called a widow for the first time, she wasn't sure to whom the reference was made. Widow? How did *we* become *me*? How did *Mrs.* become *Ms.*

Dealing with John's death was monumental. Processing the absence of their closest friend, Jackson, was unfathomable. She could never forgive him for letting John die without being by his side. He wasn't the man she had always believed him to be. Grieving John's death and Jackson's friendship was more than she could bear.

Like clockwork, the twelfth of the month circled around. The anticipation of each cycle wore on Rachel. Month nine. Month ten. Eleven. She still couldn't believe it was true. The trauma of losing John revisited her most profoundly on the monthly anniversary of his death. She thought surely all her tears had been shed. Alas, there was always one more unexpected outburst awaiting its turn just below the surface.

The one-year anniversary loomed. Rachel sat alone in complete darkness. She didn't move. Depression settled on her. On the room. On the house. All longed for the man who brought them to life. She didn't want to accept John's absence. She didn't want to hope for the future. She didn't even want to live. "Eventually, you'll start to feel better," an acquaintance assured. The statement angered Rachel. *Feel better? All I have left is the pain. My pain connects me to John. It's all I have left of him.*

Rachel awoke to the anniversary. Three hundred and sixty-five days without him.

Rachel wept until there was no energy left inside, but the tears continued. She sat on the kitchen floor with a box of tissues and her playlist. She searched until she found the song. Their song. Her phone was set to replay as she engaged the downward spiral.

Rachel revisited the night John left. When the deep sleep came, for which they had been told. It was still somehow unexpected. She and their daughters gathered close. Though the journey had been long, the end came quickly.

They gathered around while John's heart slowed. Held his hands. Thanked him for being the most amazing husband, father and Poppy. Whispered sweet salutations in his ears. Kissed him goodbye.

They bid him farewell to go to Jesus. To go to John Avery the Third, who was waiting for his daddy. They held him until his last breath—the last breath that came just five days after the doctors conveyed the news.

Rachel's heart remembered the night. Tears came without hinderance as she leaned against the table John built. Tissues soaked up her grief. One after the other. The hours passed, and her pain grew. Rachel needed to see John one more time. To touch him. To talk to him. To hold him in her arms.

What could she do to have him back for just a moment? What bargain could she make with God? She begged and pleaded. If she couldn't go back, she wouldn't allow herself to go forward. She knew this would be the day her heart stopped.

Irish whiskey! There was a bottle somewhere in the kitchen. A gift bestowed three Christmases ago. Rachel kindly accepted and then tucked it away in the back of her pantry. She had avoided alcohol. Her life experiences dictated it. The only objective now was to forget. Avoiding no longer applied. Her pain was dictating.

Rachel found it. She removed the bow and dusted off the bottle. With her paring knife, she carved out the cork. No glass was used. None needed. She returned to the floor. The song. The drink. Her tears. Rachel called for John as she consumed her relief. Begging him to come home. Just for one more of anything.

By 1 a.m., Rachel was paralyzed. Her cheek leaning into the cold wooden floor. Lights on. Song still playing. A half-empty bottle before her. Through her drunkenness, Rachel knew she was helpless.

She remembered her friend, Camille, who texted early in the evening. The youngest of her *Crazies*. She had not responded. Nothing had been allowed to interrupt her tumble down memory lane. Rachel could barely lift her head and could scarcely see her phone. She pressed the last contact. Camille answered. "I need you," Rachel whispered through her tears. "I'll be right there!"

The next thing Rachel remembered, Camille was kneeling at her side. "Let's get you to the bed." She wrapped her arms around Rachel's shoulders and gave her a gentle pull. Rachel couldn't stand. The motion disturbed the liquor inside her, turning bottom to top. Camille grabbed a trash can. The night's labor revisited in the most violent way.

Rachel awoke in her bed. Daylight had finally come, leaving behind the evening's suffering.

The emotion had settled, but the physical anguish continued. Camille had coffee and painkillers for what she knew her friend would regret quite strongly.

Together, the two friends emptied the remaining whiskey down the drain. When Camille drove away late in the morning, Rachel called the florist. Flowers were sent in gratitude for a debt Rachel could never repay. "Mrs. Avery, what would you like on the card?" Rachel waited. No words would suffice. "Just write, *Thank you for holding my hair!*"

At noon, Simon showed up at Rachel's door. "I brought dumplings. Uncle Jimmy says they're your favorite." Rachel smiled with glassy eyes. "They are. Please come in." Rachel retrieved plates, and the two sat.

"You made it through the first year. That's the toughest. All the *Firsts*." Rachel nodded. Trying to hold herself steady. Simon knew the sting of loss. His Suzanne had been gone for two years.

"How did you do on the first anniversary? I didn't call because I've been there. No one can do it for you. You just have to walk it out." Rachel gave an embarrassed look. "It wasn't my finest hour, but I made it through. Thank the Lord, I made it through!"

Chapter Nineteen

───────── ≈ ─────────

B y fall, Rachel was no longer clinging to her pain. The mid-February
night spent drowning in her sorrow seemed only a distant nightmare.
Though she committed to never taking that route again, her heart began to
shift from judgement to empathy for those who used alcohol to numb their
inconceivable pain. Her new strategy? Phone a friend first.

Grief had not departed. By no means. It had changed positions in her
life. Front and center was no longer the place it occupied. A renewal was
surfacing. A transition. Little by little. More happy days than sad days com-
posed her weeks and months.

Rachel's grief over John's life—their life—became more predictable as
time passed. No longer debilitating. She wondered how God would work all
of the turmoil and pain for her good. Would He? Could He? She believed
so. Her faith was built on that belief. To forfeit now would shift her entire
belief system. Her life's foundation. Her emotions doubted it all. Her faith
said, "*God is still working!*"

A year and a half after John's departure, Rachel's heart was beating again. She wore each month's passage like a badge of honor. A badge of survival. Her heart was healing. She finally wanted it.

In all areas except one. Jackson and Anastasia Stone. Rachel had invited a bitter seed to take root. She wanted it there. It felt good to despise them. She had harbored a desire to hate Anastasia. Now she had good cause.

Jackson had broken her heart most profoundly. Rachel felt justified in her unforgiveness. She didn't believe the gaping wound would ever heal, and she didn't care. This was an area she kept from her prayers. She knew what God would say. His words that were already spoken. She wasn't prepared to act on them. She tucked the disobedience in a secret box in her heart and closed the lid.

"Take care of Jackson!" John had requested on his final day. Rachel was angry that Jackson had not come to bid his best friend farewell after the brotherhood God created between the two. How could John even mention Jackson's name after the betrayal he executed on them? He had not shown his face to console her after John died. To be the shoulder she longed to cry on. He vanished from her life with no explanation.

Rachel began to rebuild structure in her life. She volunteered with Uncle Jimmy at the hardware store. Helped him with the livestock. She even participated in the planting in the spring. It felt right to connect with people again. To use her mind. To get her hands dirty. Having her hands in the soil was therapeutic.

She piddled in the old, established gardens of The Renaissance House. Through the spring and summer, she had pruned. All the dead limbs and branches were cut away. Weeds were pulled. Trails and walkways that had been covered for decades were finally coming into their own. Leading her into the secret alcoves created by her predecessors with azaleas, camellias and roses of Sharon of every color serving as the living walls. Walls and walkways that led to places of intimacy and peace.

Rachel was up early, attired in her Mexican Corral boots. They had been resoled at least twice. They were a must for harvesting. For farm life in general. They had survived since her first season with John and Jackson, when she was still a teenager. It was tradition.

She had her oatmeal and apple before the sun rose. The second cup of coffee was taken to the swing. As the sun filtered through the leaves, Rachel's prayer reached out from her heart. *Lord, help me move forward. Show me the way.* Before her prayers had ended, the sounds of tractors converged on the land.

Rachel watched as rows of peanuts were picked. As capacity combine hoppers unloaded into the long tractor trailer. Load after load, the mound of peanuts grew. Her eyes following the dust trails rising throughout the field created excitement for Rachel. It was a high she had missed.

She returned to the house to prepare lunch. Uncle Jimmy and the help would be ready for a homecooked meal by noon. Fried pork chops, peas, okra, corn on the cob, and cornbread—all of Uncle Jimmy's favorites. All products of the farm. Even the corn meal was ground from dried corn raised a year prior. A chocolate cream pie would top off the meal. Rachel worked steadily, glancing often at the fields behind the house. She rushed about pouring iced tea, slicing a ripe tomato and retrieving a jar of her latest batch of pepper jelly from the pantry.

Everything was in place with five minutes to spare. She walked to the backyard to flag the guys down. Both tractors were already making their way to the edge of the yard. Rachel was all smiles as the door of Uncle Jimmy's tractor cab opened. She positioned her hand above her eyes, blocking the sun's glare from her gaze. He slowly exited, moving down the ladder. Then he turned…facing Rachel. He didn't move. Rachel squinted, attempting to focus. Stepping closer, she gasped. She couldn't believe her eyes. Jackson Stone.

The two stared at each other with no words. Rachel's heart pounded. Her respiration rate increased. Emotion swelled into quiet, angry tears.

"Rachel." Jackson's tone was soft and humble. She didn't speak. Uncle Jimmy exited the second tractor and walked toward Rachel. "WHAT is he doing here?" Disdain enveloped her attitude. Uncle Jimmy approached Rachel, placing a hand on each shoulder. "Rachel, stay calm. He's here to help me." Rachel shook her head. "No! Get him off this land! Now!" She turned and rushed to the house. Jackson called out in a desperate plea. "Rachel, please!"

Before she made her way to her bedroom, she could no longer see. A well of tears clouded her view. Rachel stumbled to the bed, collapsing in her emotions. Hysterical sobs overtook her. Anger was at the forefront. As her tears flowed, a change came that she didn't expect. Her anger began to dissolve into pain, which flooded her heart. Hearing his voice. Seeing his eyes. The wound was ripped open. Holding back was not possible. The dam broke.

By the time the emotion had settled and the tears had subsided, Rachel was completely exhausted. She remained on the bed, drifting in and out of sleep. She was thankful when the chatter in the kitchen became quiet.

The tractors departed. She was glad she had avoided Jackson. She wondered why Uncle Jimmy had brought him anyway. He knew how she felt. How Jackson had hurt her. She wasn't prepared to face this.

For the next few days, the tractors hummed in the field. Rachel prepared lunch and left two plates on the back porch. She never showed her face. She couldn't. The joy she had regained plummeted. Her newly found strength was depleted. *Lord, I asked for help to move forward. He is my past.*

By the end of the week, the field had been cleared and the peanuts hauled away. Uncle Jimmy knocked at the back door at sunset. The door that was usually unlocked wasn't. Rachel stepped out on the porch and sat on the railing, looking away. "Rachel, things are not always what they seem." She turned.

"Really? My husband died never knowing why his best friend deserted him. That is JUST what it seems!"

"Actually, Rachel, no. It's not that at all." He fumbled and fidgeted. "Jackson did see John before he died."

"That is not true! I was here. Those last two days, John kept saying his name. It broke my heart."

"There's a good reason for that, Rachel. You told me the girls were taking you to a doctor's appointment and that Camille's husband, Dan, would be sitting with John for a few hours. I brought Jackson that day while you were gone. He shared with John what had happened in his life. He broke. He asked John's forgiveness for not being here for him. For you. He was only here for a few hours, then went straight back to Atlanta."

"None of us could have known John only had two days left. Not when the doctors said a few months. In the best way John could, he told Jackson there was nothing to forgive. With every ounce of strength he could muster, John sat up and embraced his friend. His hurting friend. I thank God for the timing."

Rachel began to pace. "Timing! Try almost two years! How's that for timing? I have carried heartbreak all this time. Now you tell me that the reason John was saying Jackson's name was because he was here. In MY house, and NO ONE told me."

"Rachel, I'm sorry. I'm so sorry. Sometimes there is no roadmap to navigate tragedy. You just have to figure it out one step at a time. Jackson didn't want you to know because of all you were already facing with John." Uncle Jimmy approached Rachel. With a gentle touch to her chin, he directed her face to his. "I'm asking you to trust me. Give Jackson a chance."

Rachel was restless through the night. Memories ran over and over in her mind. Her emotions were intense, and her dreams chaotic. She didn't want her mind to circle back to the low places, but in the night, her pain was magnified. Then there was the weight of John's final words. Words that echoed in her mind. "Take care of Jackson." Rachel wondered how she could trust him. For almost two years, she had suffered under his absence.

Daylight arrived through her window. Rachel clung to the covers. Hiding her face. She had not found rest until the wee hours of the morning. Her mind wouldn't allow it. Her body's dead weight refused to move.

It was afternoon before Rachel could force herself out of her pajamas to shower and dress. Her gardenia garden was all that could convince her to leave the house. Even with blooms long gone. She settled into her swing, taking in the views she loved. The field harvested earlier in the week was now sprinkled with large, round bales of peanut hay. Serving as the backdrop to The Renaissance House, it could have been a painting.

The sun settled above the opposing horizon, and she into the rhythm of the swing. The repeated creak of the rubbing chains, in concert with the gentle glide, lured Rachel to rest. She lowered her back to the swing and closed her eyes. One foot on the ground, perpetuating the motion.

The silence was broken by the sound of a closing door. Rachel sat up.

Her heart began to race. It was Jackson. He moved toward her with confidence. His eyes were set on hers. She wanted to run, but her gaze was locked on him. *God, give me strength.* She watched his stride until he was standing before her. "May I join you?" Rachel glanced down at the empty seat beside her. Jackson lowered his frame.

The two sat with no words between them. The swing rocked back and forth as the minutes passed. Jackson lifted his arm, wrapping it over Rachel's shoulder and pulling her toward him.

She didn't resist. She melted into his embrace. It was the most comfort she had felt since John died.

Jackson reached down, slipping his fingers under Rachel's chin. He raised her face with the slightest motion until her eyes met his. "Rachel, I'm sorry." Anguish settled in his blue eyes. "I'm so sorry for not being here for you. I'm truly sorry." His voice began to quiver. "Will you—can you—forgive me? Please forgive me." He pulled Rachel closer. Into his full embrace. Both arms holding her against his body. Her face nestled against his neck. She breathed him in and didn't move. Almost two years of anger melted away, breath by breath.

Rachel wanted to stay in his embrace. Near his heart. It felt too good to move. She remained for a few moments, then lifted her head to respond. "Jackson!" She was startled. "Look!" He turned to see smoke rising from the edge of the wood line. The two jumped up and began racing toward the patch of trees. Through the field, toward the white billow. Just as the sun was disappearing into the horizon at their backs, the full moon cast its luminance over their path.

The closer Jackson and Rachel found themselves to the trees, the more the cloud vanished. As quickly as it appeared, it was gone. The two stopped. They looked at each other. Then the trees. They were speechless. There was no explanation.

The two stood on the ridge in the middle of the acreage. The night had fallen with haste. The moon was their lamp. The early evening temperature was mild. Rachel plopped down to settle her breathlessness. Jackson beside her. "A cloud. A cloud emerged, then disappeared. Wow! That was unusual!" Jackson scratched his head. "Yep. I can't explain that! But here we are... following a cloud? Maybe divine intervention!"

He turned to Rachel. "Before you answer my question, I want to share my story. I wanted more than anything in the world for you to know. To tell you everything. When you messaged about John's last MRI report, I just couldn't do it. I couldn't add to your struggle. I would rather carry the load alone than add even one more burden for you."

"Jackson, I don't understand. What could be so bad that kept you from us? I assumed it was Anastasia. She's never accepted our friendship." Jackson nodded. "Yes. It was Anastasia. Just not what you think.

"It was February 9. The day of John's appointment and Dr. and Mrs. Blevins' 40th anniversary. We spent the night with my parents the night before. We planned to join Anastasia's mom and dad for brunch at ten o'clock at their lake house.

"Anastasia wanted to take the car around the lake. I convinced her that we should take the boat. It was a beautiful morning. 'It's not just about the destination. Let's enjoy the journey.' She agreed under duress. She was lying down on the back bench seat, reading a magazine, when we started the short trip.

"As I rounded the last cape before the Blevins' property, a flock of Canada geese had just gone airborne. I yelled out to Anastasia to hold on. I throttled back pretty strong to miss them. I heard a commotion and turned to see Anastasia on the floor. She wasn't moving. She had fallen off the bench. Her head hit Dad's metal toolbox. She was unconscious.

"It was a whirlwind from there. From the Blevins' home, her dad had her life flighted to Emory, where the top neurologist was waiting. A neurosurgeon on standby. Besides the obvious injury to her head, there were no other signs of trauma.

"I wasn't allowed to leave with the family. The Gainesville police came to interview me. I had to take a breathalyzer. There were lots of questions about why we took the boat instead of driving. Had we been having marital problems? Did we have an argument that morning? You name it, they asked. It was like a criminal investigation. I'm thankful my parents were there with me. I just wanted to get to the hospital."

The moon rose higher as the two sat huddled together. Compassion began to move in Rachel's heart. She put an arm around Jackson's back. With the other, she looped her fingers in his. She remained quiet.

"It was late afternoon before I got to Emory. A CT scan was done as soon as she arrived at the hospital. The concussion was labeled as very severe. She remained unconscious for five days. I stayed by her side except for the hours it took to visit John. The Blevins were cool and distant. I didn't realize until later that they blamed me. If I had not insisted we take the boat—" Rachel stopped him. "Jackson, it was an accident!"

"The worse came later. When Anastasia awoke, everyone was ecstatic. There seemed to be no neurological deficits. Besides a severe headache and nausea that subsided days later, all seemed normal. Except one thing. Her memory. She remembered everything and everyone in her life. Except me. She had no idea who I was. The doctor said it could be temporary and that only time would tell. I went to the bathroom and vomited and cried and vomited some more. I couldn't believe it.

"Anastasia was one hundred percent herself. Her relationships were just fine. You wouldn't even know she had been injured. But she had no memory of her husband. No memory that she ever had a husband or anything that happened after we met. In one moment, in one twist of fate, everything changed.

"Anastasia was released seven days after her hospitalization. Her parents took her to their Buckhead home. I stayed too but was asked to take a different bedroom. Which I did, of course. Eventually, they asked if I would stay in our studio apartment and just visit her. Then it was suggested that it might be better for her if I only visited one day a week. Without warning, she asked me to stop visiting. I was methodically expelled from their lives. The next thing I knew, I received divorce papers. She never recovered any memories of me.

"The divorce was final over a year ago. I left my job at Emory around the same time. Losing John. My marriage. You. It was all more than I could handle. I was just trying to survive. As time passed, I became more and more ashamed that I hadn't contacted you. Over the last few months, John's words kept echoing in my mind. 'Take care of Rachel.'" She turned with surprise. "Rachel, I wasn't sure you ever wanted to see me again. I just had to try."

Rachel stood. She reached for Jackson's hands and pulled him up. "Jackson, I want to ask if you will forgive me for the feelings I've harbored against you. And for not being there when you needed me. I should have checked on you." A smile enveloped Jackson's whole face. He winked and reached up, scattering Rachel's hair. They both laughed.

The two canvassed the field, which was illuminated by moonlight. "What a beautiful night for a reunion, Jackson Stone. And a full moon to boot!" Jackson looked up to the sky. "It's even more special than that, Rachel. This is a blue moon." She looked up with a questioning tilt.

Jackson stepped toward Rachel. He could see that the lowering evening temperature had given her a chill. He pulled open his jacket and nodded at her, motioning her toward him. She slid her hands inside, moving them around his waist. She leaned into his warm frame.

"A blue moon is rare. One will come only every two or three years. It is the second full moon that occurs in one calendar month. It's where we get the saying, *Once in a blue moon*. A truly rare event." Rachel gazed at Jackson, taking in the details she had never seen before this night and soaking in the depth of his voice. "Once in a blue moon, something special...or someone special... can come into your life." He looked down into her eyes. With a gentle touch of his hands, he held her face in place. "Or maybe...twice!" He lowered himself to her lips.

Chapter Twenty

---≈---

Jackson and Rachel were inseparable. They picked up where they left off. Their friendship was stronger than ever, and something new was blooming. They were thankful for John's blessing. The way he directed them toward one another. They shared their sorrow and grief, which they held from each other for too long. The words came easily now. The two visited John's grave. Jackson wept.

Rounds were made through their old stomping grounds. They dropped in at the hardware store and worked with Uncle Jimmy for a few hours. Seeing remnants still carrying John's handwriting brought smiles.

They fished. Hunted dove in the empty peanut field. Drove the old country roads. They sat in the swing, remembering the last Christmas. How Jackson carried out John's wish for Rachel's swing without her knowing. Their lives were intertwined in the most beautiful way.

Just a few weeks into October, the two were embracing their second chance. Neither was afraid of the transition. Each was thankful for it. This season of life was different than spring and summer. More life lay behind them than before. They were ready. The fire was lit.

The flame was growing.

It felt good to experience happiness again. To have companionship. To not be alone. Both knew the sting of love and loss. Starting over was not easy. With a best friend, it was certainly advantageous.

Rachel wasn't planning a party this year for Jackson's birthday. After a few weeks among friends of New Berry, she wanted him all to herself. They went out for a steak dinner, as he requested. Jackson's favorite dessert was chilling at The Renaissance House.

The couple sat on the front porch, wrapped in a blanket that cut the chill of the autumn breeze. Rachel shared how she had let out a few rooms in the detached section of the house throughout the year. Just to keep busy. "I've been working on transitioning to a bed and breakfast. I planned to start after Christmas. Family will be in and out during the holiday. I think January is good timing. I still have some work to do. Locks for the bedroom doors. Handrails for the steps. I'm working on it a little at a time." Jackson chimed in. "I know a very good carpenter. He has pretty good rates. I could put in a good word for you." Rachel rolled her eyes. "Ha! I'm sure." He leaned over, kissing the top of her head.

"When I left the hospital, I worked with my dad. I didn't realize how much I missed being with him day in and day out. He's such a good guy. I've enjoyed getting my hands dirty again. Supervising was great, don't get me wrong. But there is nothing like having tools in your hands. Creating something you can be proud of. Something lasting."

"I agree. When I am creative, when I create something of value, it makes me feel like I'm taking after my father...my Heavenly Father. You know... THE Creator."

"Wow! I never thought of it that way. But yes! I want to start my own company. Build some houses. Not in Georgia. I can't live there. You know... the water...the bridge...water under...water over...water everywhere. Too much hard life was lived there."

"Jackson, there's no reason to move back there. You love it here. Your parents do, too. New Berry has always been your home." Rachel stood and began to fold the blanket. "Now! Time for dessert. Instead of a cake, I made your favorite. Chocolate Delight!" Jackson perked up. "With the baked pecan crust? With layers of sweetened cream cheese, chocolate pudding and Cool Whip?" Rachel laughed. "Yep, that's the one." Jackson jumped up. "Dang, let's go!"

Rachel changed into something a little more comfortable and pulled her hair up off her neck. She entered the kitchen with Jackson, who was waiting patiently. He looked at her and took a deep breath. "What? Why are you looking at me that way?" Jackson stepped closer. "Even in sweats and a hair clip, you're beautiful." Rachel blushed. "Thank you. A double helping for you!"

She served a bowl and hopped up on the kitchen counter. Jackson's six foot five frame still towered over her. "You! Come here!" She pointed at him, then motioned with her finger for him to join her. "What is that mischievous grin about? Am I safe?" Rachel raised an eyebrow, shooting a flirtatious look across the room. Then she laughed out loud. "Maybe."

Jackson stood before Rachel. She dipped a mouthful of dessert onto the spoon and directed it to his mouth. He took it in. "Hmmm. This is delicious! Who needs birthday cake!" She offered another bite. "I'm glad you like it." Jackson leaned in a little closer. She offered more. As he leaned in, she pulled the spoon back and ate the bite herself. "Hey now! Watch out!"

Their eyes locked. The chemistry between them was satisfying. Jackson leaned in, kissing Rachel's cheek. She wrapped her foot behind his thigh and pulled him closer. She offered another bite, then leaned forward, kissing his lips. Before Rachel could pull away from the kiss, Jackson scooped her off the counter. She began to laugh and protest. "Too late now!" Jackson teased.

He carried her to the couch and dropped her there. The laughter paused as he lowered his knee to the cushion and leaned in, pressing his lips to hers. She welcomed his kiss. The affection unfolded as the two embraced. Rachel sighed as Jackson ran his fingers firmly across the back of her neck and into her hair.

As the two yielded to their emotions, Rachel's phone alerted. Jackson sat up immediately, taking his place on the end of the couch. He ran his fingers through his waves, moving them back in place. "What was that? Your Bible app?" Rachel burst out in laughter. "Whew! Rachel, that was intense! In the most amazing way! Intense!" Rachel picked up her phone. "It's your mom. You obviously didn't answer her last message." Jackson leaned back, tilting his head. "Way to go, Patsy! Gotta love her!" He smiled at Rachel as he wiped perspiration from his forehead.

"Rachel, I'm sorry. I know this was not appropriate. Even though we're adults. I never want to disrespect you. I'm very sorry."

"I'm sorry as well. It takes two. I'm not going to lie. I want to be intimate with you. I do. But more than that, I want us to keep our relationship with God first. One day, in His time, under His conditions, we can enjoy a passionate relationship the way He intends. With no holding back. For now, we will obviously have to be more careful."

"You're right, Rachel. No more Chocolate Delight for us!"

Thanksgiving brought all three Avery families home. They were thrilled to have Jackson back in their lives. Somehow, it made missing their dad less sharp. Jackson had always been a second dad to Jacq, Faith and Beth. Now he was standing in... with John's blessing. Jackson knew his way around the house and the farm. Rachel had forgotten how wonderful it was to have a companion share the load. The two worked in perfect sync. They even finished each other's sentences.

Jackson was in his element. He couldn't get enough of John and Rachel's grandkids. He rode them around the fields on the Gator. Piled in. Just as John would have. Giggles rang out from the tiny bodies. Jackson shared stories of Poppy that only he could tell. Some only a best friend would know. Jacq, Faith and Beth listened with tear-filled eyes and smiles.

He filled in just as he knew John would want. He even gathered the whole family for a visit to the cemetery. Flowers were placed by the grandchildren. Avery, who was born the week John died and was the first-born boy in Mr. Avery's line since John's birth fifty years earlier, left his toy next to the flowers. A tiny metal peanut wagon. He nodded and smiled. As if he knew that Poppy knew. Precious memories were made, and more healing came for all.

When the family gathered around the table, tears filled Jackson's eyes. He looked toward heaven. "We will always miss you, my Friend." His prayer went forth, and the family engaged in their traditional Thanksgiving meal.

Rachel opened the door. The sun had barely topped the horizon. "Good morning! Merry Christmas!" Jackson leaned in against the door post, delivering a long, soft kiss to Rachel's cheek. A bouquet of gardenias in hand. "Since they are out of season, I preordered from the florist. Just for you!" His eyes were like fire to her soul. She took the bouquet and breathed in the sweetness of the white blooms and the scent of this man, whom she now loved in a brand-new way.

The house was decorated a little less than usual. The girls were spending Christmas with their in-laws. Thanksgiving in New Berry. Christmas away. The following year, they would be home for Christmas. That was their way. Exchanging holidays. Sharing the love.

"Wrap up! Let's swing a bit. The temperature is mild today." Rachel retrieved her coat and scarf. Jackson poured hot cups of coffee. Heading down the steps, Rachel looped her arm around his. The camellias had especially abundant blooms this year. They were breathtaking. When they arrived at the swing, Jackson spread a blanket over it, and then Rachel sat. She laid her head on Jackson's shoulder and expelled a satisfying sigh.

"Uncle Jimmy is cooking a big lunch. The smells coming out of that kitchen! He's expecting us at noon."

"Great! I'm looking forward to it. I've prepared a light breakfast to tide us over."

"Rachel, I want us to spend a few moments in our special place. To give you your Christmas gifts here. I couldn't think of a better spot."

"Ok." She looked around. "I don't see anything. Where are they?"

Jackson reached inside his jacket, pulled out a small flat box and placed it in Rachel's hands.

Rachel tore away the paper. Opening the box, she lifted four tea-stained dinner napkins beautifully embroidered with the formal letter *S*. Rachel glanced at Jackson, conveying her confusion. He reached inside his jacket once more and retrieved a tiny, blue velvet box.

"Rachel, I've loved you since the beginning. Though I would have never acted on that love inappropriately. John knew how I felt. He always knew. He found great pleasure in teasing me when we were younger. 'How could you not love her? I'm just glad I found her first.' He actually thought it was kind of sweet." Rachel smiled. "I'm glad you both thought so highly of me. What's not to love? Bossy. Opinionated. Independent. Stubborn." Jackson put his finger over Rachel's lips, silencing her.

"I consider myself blessed to have known both of you and to have enjoyed the friendship of a lifetime. The napkins were my grandmother's. She and Pop were together for sixty-five years. They passed them to Mom and Dad on their wedding day. Now they are passing them to us." Jackson dropped to one knee. Rachel's eyes widened.

"Rachel, I love you with all my heart. Friendship is no longer enough for me." He opened the hinged box to display a solitaire ruby engagement ring ornately set in white gold. Rachel pulled her hands to her face, covering her mouth in complete surprise. Holding her breath. "I want to be with you, only you, for the rest of my life. Will you marry me?"

Rachel poured Sam a cup of coffee and placed it next to her breakfast plate. "How did you sleep? Was everything in your room to your liking? Sam swallowed a bite of French toast and patted her mouth with her monogrammed napkin. "Yes, ma'am! I slept like a baby. I woke up early and enjoyed a walk through the garden. I sat in the swing a while." She took a sip of coffee. "Your gardenias are blooming. Spring is in the air. I was amazed how much you can see from that spot." Rachel filled the juice glass a second time. "I'm so glad you slept well. Enjoy your breakfast. Let me know if you need anything." She turned and headed back to the kitchen.

"Ms. Rachel, I've been over the moon thinking about the proposal that happened in the very spot where I sat. I've been running your story over and over in my head. I'd love to meet Jackson. And to hear about your wedding. Will you share it with me?"

Rachel stopped in her tracks. Her look turned stoic. With hesitation, she turned back. She walked to the table, taking a seat across from Sam. She leaned in on her elbows in contemplation. "I suppose a wedding would be the obvious assumption." Rachel looked into the gathering room at the engagement picture taken the week after Christmas the previous year. Just four months earlier. "Yes, I'll share. Then I need to get started on lunch. Planting starts today.

"Jackson and I were never married." Shock dropped on Sam's face. "What? What do you mean? You were so in love! Everything was perfect! Why? What happened?" Rachel pushed away from the table and approached the window that looked toward her gardenia garden. "Everything WAS perfect. Then it wasn't. As quickly as it came, it was gone."

Rachel and Jackson sat at the long farm table, working side by side. Rachel was designing breakfast menus for The Renaissance House Bed & Breakfast while Jackson designed their home. Their dream home he would build just beyond the ridge on the bank of the pond. Periodically, they glanced at each other. Laughter would erupt. Neither could believe how happiness had visited them so fully.

Rachel was distracted from her work. She kept scrolling back through the proofs she had received just that morning. The engagement session with Sarah and Ben in the Scotts' hay field made it real. Jackson's black suit hung perfectly, enunciating the broadness of his shoulders. Rachel's vintage dress, found at a local antique shop, was her style *to a tee*. Handmade in Mexico.

The session was Jackson's idea. He wanted every step of their journey memorialized. Middle-aged or not, their love was fresh and new and alive. Well wishes had been steadily arriving since Sarah posted the couple on their studio website. "No turning back now." They agreed in jest. The word was out.

Jackson's phone rang. "Happy New Year, Dad! Did you and mom make it until the ball dropped last night?" Jackson retreated. His look was suddenly serious and somber. "What is it, Dad? I'm going to put you on speaker for Rachel." He laid the phone on the table. "Good morning, Mr. Stone." No greeting was returned. "Jackson...Rachel...I have news. I don't really know how to tell you this." Jackson and Rachel locked eyes, waiting.

"Is it Mom?"

"No, Jackson. I'm right here. I'm fine."

"Dad, what is it? What's wrong?"

"I got a call from Dr. Blevins early this morning. It appears...it appears Anastasia regained her memory. She remembers you, Jackson!" Jackson's jaw dropped. The color drained from his face. He was dumbfounded. Rachel tried to process the announcement. The words couldn't make it beyond her disbelief.

"She has asked to see you, Jackson."

Chapter Twenty-One

———≋———

A jolt roused Rachel from her sleep. "Madam, are you ok? The steward lingered. "I'm fine. First time flying." He smiled and patted Rachel on the shoulder. "Once we hit cruising altitude, the flight will be smoother. Let me know if you need anything. Anything at all." He continued down the aisle of the Boeing 747. Turbulence had shaken her from her dream. More appropriately, her nightmare.

The days before Jackson's departure from New Berry played over and over like a movie. Anastasia wanted to see Jackson. Most assuredly, she wanted him back. With all the protests he delivered—with confirmations that he didn't love Anastasia anymore—Rachel still wouldn't relent. He had to return to Atlanta to face his ex-wife. He wasn't the kind of man to walk away from unfinished business. Even under grueling circumstances.

Rachel was assured of the love she and Jackson shared. She knew he wanted to marry her. To begin their new life. To leave behind his past. It was the agony deep in his eyes that she couldn't deny. The moral dilemma vexed him.

Jackson wouldn't easily concede to returning to Atlanta. Not until Rachel removed her engagement ring and folded it in the palm of his hand. "I love you with all my heart. Don't doubt that. But you have to go. We both know you have to go."

Pushing Jackson back toward Atlanta was the right thing to do, no matter how much they loved one another. No matter the degree of hope that had to be pushed aside. Rachel had not shed a single tear since she watched Jackson's tail lights disappear from the farm. A switch flipped inside her. A numbness fell over her heart. A week ago seemed like a lifetime.

Turbulence once again shook the aircraft. Rachel closed her eyes and gripped the armrests. She tried not to think about ascending 35,000 feet above the ground. Air, nothing but air beneath her. She understood the principles of *lift*. She had even taught them in her science class. It all made perfect sense...in the textbook...in theory. It was trusting the truths in real time that was her struggle.

In this season, she was struggling to trust God's truth too. To believe when she couldn't see. To have faith in Him. How could God allow the circumstances she faced? How could He possibly work all of this out for good? Rachel's heart was too tired to even imagine it.

She caught her second flight to Iquitos after a short layover in Lima. The sights and sounds were all new. She embraced them. She spent a lifetime listening to John and Jackson's stories, thumbing through their photos, and watching the videos they captured. Living it was different. If she closed her eyes, she could remember their voices. Their unmatched excitement. Opportunities to serve touched the deepest parts of their souls. Now, Rachel was compelled to seek out what she had only known from a distance.

She was happy to finally be on the ground. To lay eyes on Kaye and Tucker. They retrieved her from the airport and headed to their home in the Punchana Region. At an early hour, she would be cast forth on her Amazon journey with her hired longboat driver. Kaye and Tucker insisted on accompanying her, but Rachel refused. She needed to go alone. The villagers were not expecting her. That was what she preferred. By nightfall, she would be back in Punchana.

Tucker had reserved the most reputable driver and their personal friend. His daily trip, motoring up and down the river, passed by the loading bank of the village. Rachel traveled only with a backpack with a few changes of clothes. Appropriate for a day's journey during the erratic rainy season.

Rachel sat in seclusion during the morning voyage in her poncho and waterproof boots. She took in all the views and movement along the waterway. She watched the people who periodically emerged on the riverbanks. As she arrived at her destination, the driver tied the boat off and climbed out. He pulled Rachel to the top of the embankment to the village trail. Balancing on planks laid end to end. "I pray, Ms. Avery. For you."

His face winced. Tears gathered in his eyes. He patted his chest. "My friend, John. Mi amigo!" Rachel reached out, taking the gentleman's hand. He knew John. She could see his pain. "I go village, Ms. Avery." Rachel conceded. She couldn't resist. His heart was full of friendship for John. He wanted to deliver her safely. They walked the mile mostly in silence. Photos could have never conveyed the deep friendship she saw in his eyes. Why would they not love John? He was so easy to love.

As they topped the plateau, Rachel froze. She rotated her body full circle to absorb every view. Her heart had recorded John's descriptions. She remembered his words. Now it was before her. She watched the people moving about. It was all familiar yet brand new.

A villager spotted the woman standing by the Peruvian. She yelled out to the others, who turned to see Rachel. She heard her name among the commotion that was building. Somehow, she was not a stranger to them.

The pastor exited the church, looking her way. Assurance emerged on his face. The children and adults alike began to rush toward Rachel in celebration. Even the guide joined in. They called out her name over and over. *Ms. Avery! Ms. Avery!* How could they know? As they reached Rachel, they embraced her. The children reached up, touching her golden hair. All the while lifting praises to God.

The crowd moved in sync, almost like an army of ants. Before they reached the church, a deluge of rain dropped on them all. The second of the morning. Under the church porch, Pastor Carlos addressed Rachel. "We are so glad you are finally here!" Rachel wasn't sure how to respond. "What do you mean? I told no one I was coming." He chuckled.

An elderly lady made her way with an umbrella in one hand and a cane in the other through the mud and rain from a nearby hut. "Ms. Avery, I would like to introduce Maria. She has been telling me for weeks you were coming." Maria looped her arm around Rachel and pulled her in the direction from which she had come. "How did she know? I didn't even know then." Maria reached up, putting her hand over Rachel's heart. "God told her in a dream. She's been praying for you. For your heart."

Maria led Rachel back to her home through the shallow trenches of flowing water. Rain on and off for months made movement difficult. The villagers were not bothered. Maria pulled back the door frame, covered in rusty tin. With apprehension, Rachel entered.

Oil lanterns lit the room, which was divided by a curtain hung from wall to wall. It displayed beautiful hand-embroidered pictures of jungle flowers. Maria's handiwork. The floor was elevated just enough to allow water to flow underneath, yet low enough so that Maria could come and go with ease.

The home was simple, with unexpected touches. A wide wooden bench sat along the wall. Seating by day and a bed at night. Pieces of clothing hung on a coat rack secured in the corner. Aged rugs adorned both areas. A small table positioned near the door. Two mismatched chairs underneath.

A decorative wash bowl with a matching water pitcher sat on its own stand. Above it was a string clipped with photos. There among the few was a photo of John, Jackson, Maria and an older gentleman huddled closely. It was Sulay. A matching picture hung in the office at The Renaissance House.

John and Sulay had loved each other as father and son for many years. Now both were gone. Maria had aged much since the photo. Rachel had not recognized her. She turned and embraced her host, so thankful to be in her home. To finally know her. Maria pointed out the picture of John and Rachel with their whole family. The third was of Jackson and Anastasia. Rachel released a soft, emotional sigh and turned away. Not wanting her host to sense her disapproval.

Within a few hours, the rain lifted. Rachel, attired in dry clothing, headed back to the church to talk to Pastor Carlos. "How do the people know me? They all called my name as if I had been here before. I haven't!" Pastor Carlos opened the door of the church and gestured Rachel in. "There's something you should see."

He led Rachel towards the back of the church building, which now had windows and storm shutters. An extension had been added to include two classrooms and a small storage room that doubled as an office for the pastor. "Rachel, John and Jackson were a part of our family. The improvements they made for our village changed our lives. They gave freely. They loved deeply."

He stopped and turned to Rachel. "The reason the people of our village were calling your name is because they do know you. The reason for their celebration when you arrived is because they have been praying for years that you would come. Come and let me show you." As the two entered a classroom, Rachel's knees went weak. She leaned against the wall, steadying herself.

She couldn't believe her eyes. Pictures covered the wall. She was in each one. "Our village prayed for you and your family. Twenty-nine years of pictures. Twenty-nine years of prayers. It was John and Jackson's greatest desire that you come here. Today, the people celebrated God's answer." Maria joined the two in the classroom.

"Sulay and Maria loved John. He reminded them of their son. Their son lost too soon. John always brought them something to make their lives a little easier or made something for them while he was here. A bench. A table. Even a raised floor. We miss our brother. But we will see him again one day."

Rachel turned to Maria and began to weep. Maria embraced Rachel as a mother would a child. She felt her loss. Her life was void of John...and Jackson. Maria knew the pain of profound loss. She had lived it.

The love Rachel felt in this place, in this moment, from these people, God's people, washed over her wounded soul. It was a warm ointment that soothed the pain. Maria held Rachel and prayed in words she didn't understand. Rachel cherished the way God had moved on her behalf. How He spoke to a widow twenty-five hundred miles from her home...where her heart was broken. There were no bounds to God's love. Neither in time nor space.

Rachel couldn't pull herself away from the village. All gathered under the cover of the church, bringing their own dinner to share with her. It was a feast. "Thank you all for loving John. You changed his life." She looked around the table, scanning the faces. "Thank you for the prayers that have held me during my life. Thank you for loving me." As Pastor Carlos translated, the people rejoiced.

Before Maria and Rachel retired to the hut for the night, the people gathered around the altar to pray once again for her. The children pressed in. Young and old prayed fervently. Maria enlisted Pastor Carlos' translations once more.

"As you return to your home, all will be well. Your joy will return, and you will have a double portion. God is still working everything for your good. His promise still lives." A peace settled over Rachel. She knew she would make it through.

By planting season, Rachel had been in business for three months. Keeping busy was good. The Renaissance House stayed booked. She missed Jackson and was still very much in love with him. She never verbalized his name and tried not to think about his second chance with Anastasia. She couldn't let her mind go there. Her emotions required tight reins.

Rachel blocked off reservations for planting week, but not before one guest booked a room. A single female completing a research project at Fort Redding. Rachel left it. One guest wouldn't hinder.

She was up early, making breakfast for Samantha, or Sam, as her guest requested. It was Thursday. Thursday was the *Stella Rose* breakfast. French toast, bacon, scrambled eggs and fresh fruit. There was now a grandchild for every day of the week. A breakfast was named for each one of them.

Rachel smiled, remembering their little voices asking, "Is it my day, Mimi?" when the family visited the prior month. Rachel made each child a dedicated menu. It created a full morning. Their smiles and giggles were worth it.

When Sam finished her meal, Rachel immediately began cleaning the breakfast dishes. Before the young researcher exited the house for her appointment at Fort Redding, she paused and embraced Rachel. Rachel could see Sam had been touched by the pain of her loss. "I'm sorry about Jackson. I'm so sorry, Ms. Rachel."

Lunch preparations began right away. Uncle Jimmy came in at noon on the dot with a red clay hue about him. Sam was giddy when she arrived back at The Renaissance House to find Uncle Jimmy at the table. The stories Rachel shared came to life in his presence.

"I feel as if I am meeting a movie star." Uncle Jimmy's laugh bellowed. "Well, I've never been called that before! Don't get your hopes too high, young lady! We're just common folk around here!" Sam exited again for a few more hours of work. She would return late in the afternoon, not wanting to miss her last homemade treat.

After breakfast and lunch dishes were cleaned and returned to their appropriate places, Rachel laid out ingredients for her afternoon baking. She then retreated to her bedroom.

Sharing her story with Sam created a sense of heaviness. It was like reliving the events. She drifted off to sleep with the sounds of tractors in the distance. The seeds were going into the ground. *Help me start over, Lord. Help me grow something new in my life.*

The alarm sounded. Rachel shook off her brief sleep and went about her afternoon chores. She gave the bouquet of gardenias a fresh drink of water. Jackson's memory still accompanied every breath of their scent she captured. Cookies were placed under the glass dome.

"Ms. Rachel. I have my bags packed. Thank you for letting me stay beyond checkout. I'll be leaving right after dark. That will give me plenty of time to make my flight. You've really gone out of your way for me. I'll never forget it."

"Sam, it was my pleasure. I liked having company. I thought I wanted to be all alone during planting week. It's very sentimental for me. Emotional. You were a godsend. I needed you here." Sam perked up her shoulders and nodded her head toward her host. "My pleasure!"

Rachel stood near the edge of the field, her eyes following the movement of the tractors and the dust trails. The newly planted field looked clean and fresh. She would be counting down the days until green sprouts peaked through the ground. If this were the only *new* in her life, she would accept it.

Uncle Jimmy's tractor made its way to the yard. The door of the cab was thrown open. For a moment, Rachel froze. Her heart remembered a moment just like this. Just seven months earlier. She held her breath. A man she loved, in fact, descended. Uncle Jimmy. Rachel shook her head. She wondered why she was doing this to herself. *Let it go, Rachel!*

"I'm finished with this field. I was going to head out, but I wasn't sure if you realized...you have company." Rachel nodded. "Yes, Sam will be here a few more hours. She has a late flight." Uncle Jimmy glanced toward the front of the yard. "I think we are talking about different company." He smiled so big that his crooked tooth emerged. The two moved to the edge of the barn. A familiar pickup was parked in the side yard.

She turned back to Uncle Jimmy with a look of shock and uncertainty. "What do you think he is doing here?" Uncle Jimmy took a gentle grip on Rachel's shoulders. "There's only ONE way to find out." He turned her body in the direction of her gardenia garden and gave her a soft push. Rachel wanted to run to the swing, but her body refused.

Uncle Jimmy entered the house where Lane and Patsy Stone were peering out of the window. Side by side with Sam. He greeted his friends and joined them. The anticipation of the audience grew as Rachel passed the blooming bottle brush and rounded the pecan tree, just taking on its shade.

When Jackson and Rachel were in full view of each other, he knelt, pulling a single gardenia bloom. He walked to Rachel, holding the flower before her. Her eyes were big, and her breathing hard and labored.

"Everything was dealt with appropriately."

Rachel's lip began to quiver.

"I knew right away that Anastasia didn't remember me. Nor did she want me. But I saw something I had never seen in her eyes. Fear. She has never been afraid of anything. In the face of the unknown in her life, she reverted to what she knew. To what was familiar. Manipulation.

"When she saw our posted engagement pictures, she hatched a plan to interfere. Dr. and Mrs. Blevins and I had a long talk with her. She has agreed to talk to a counselor who can help her move into her new life unafraid."

"I called that same day to share. You were on a plane to Peru." He grinned ear to ear, shaking his head. "I'm so proud of your bravery. For harnessing your fear. I decided right then and there that the next time I set foot in New Berry, it would be forever. I spent the last months getting my affairs in order."

"We're yours. We're here forever. We're never going back. New Berry is our home." He took Rachel's hands. "You are my home!"

"We? What do you mean, we?" Jackson looked over Rachel's head, pointing to the house.

She turned to see Lane and Patsy Stone smiling at her. Sam and Uncle Jimmy stood alongside, equally excited. All glaring from the windows toward the couple. It was a beautiful sight. She giggled. "Oh...we!"

"If you will have us."

The onlookers stared in silence. Frozen. Waiting.

As Rachel reached up, placing her hands firmly on Jackson's cheeks and pulling him in for a kiss, The Renaissance House exploded with cheers.

Jackson and Rachel lay on the couch at the end of their workday. Basking in the glow of the Christmas tree lights. Remnants of sawdust on his slacks. The aroma of Renaissance cookies on her breath. Wrapped around one another. Side by side. Fingers intertwined. Legs wrapped over and under. Just as newlyweds should be. "It finally came in the mail today. From Sam. I wanted us to open it together." Rachel pulled the long tab on the corrugated envelope and retrieved a note.

Mrs. Rachel,

> *This is the final copy. I hope you love it as much as I do.*

> *My first book! I spent years researching for other writers. Too afraid to venture out to write a book myself. I guess I was waiting for the perfect story.*

> *I'm thankful it was yours.*

Sam

Rachel lifted the book from the envelope. She sighed at the emotion captured on the cover.

Blue Moon Rising. Jackson and Rachel shared a look of satisfaction and assurance. "Do I get to choose the actor who plays me in the movie?"

Both laughed out loud. "Sure, but you and I will do our own Chocolate Delight scene."

With the book in hand, Rachel arose from their embrace and approached the mantle. Her eyes focused on the details of the aged photo resting in its hand-hewn frame. It now sat front and center on *their* mantle. The perfect vintage wedding gift bestowed by her dear Uncle Jimmy.

Three dust-covered friends stood in a huddle in front of a rusty peanut wagon. Full of hopes and dreams and unfailing love for one another. *Best Friends.* The three had lived much life since that day. Through it all, their God remained faithful.

Jackson joined Rachel, stepping in close behind. "We miss you, John Avery. We never could have made it here without you. We can't wait for the day we see you again."

THE END

BLUE MOON
RISING

Study Companion for
Groups and Individuals

A discussion question/reflection has been provided for each chapter. Customize your study by choosing appropriate topics based on the needs of your group or use each discussion question as an individual reflection resource.

SPOILER ALERT:

Choose from chapter topics. Content of
questions may reveal unexpected story line.

Chapter One: Casting Your Care on Him

John and Rachel find themselves facing the unthinkable. During their greatest challenge, God's Word is their comfort. In Matthew 11:28-30, Jesus calls John and Rachel, and us, to bring our weariness, our burdens, to Him. Are you in a place where you are weary and burdened? Do rest and peace seem far away? We were never meant to carry the burdens alone. Jesus promises if we yoke our lives to Him, He will give us rest. Do you need to exchange a burden for *rest* in Him?

> *Heavenly Father, Today I give you _____. I surrender this burden to you. Show me how to follow you and give me strength to trust. I ask for rest that only you can give. In Jesus Name, Amen.*

Chapter Two: Trusting God's Promise

God promised to send a man who would love Rachel and share a life of purpose. He promised to work her brokenness for good as she loved Him and was called according to His purpose as reflected in Romans 8:28. However, life taught Rachel to fear and to doubt that good would come or that it would last.

Do you find it hard to believe that God's promises are for you? Has life taught you to believe that His promises are too good to be true. In what area(s) of your life do you need to see God's promises fulfilled? In what area(s) do you need Him to work all together for good?

Heavenly Father, I love you. Because I am called according to Your purpose, I ask you to take _____ and work it for good. I will trust you while I wait. In Jesus Name, Amen.

Chapter Three: Leaning into the Good Shepherd

A young Rachel is drawn to the stained glass portrayal of the Good Shepherd with a little lamb leaning naturally against him. It is the obvious trust the lamb possesses that pulls at Rachel's heart. Though she has never experienced complete trust with a man, she recognizes it, even longs for it.

Have rejection, abandonment, abuse, betrayal caused a pattern of mistrust in your life? Is it difficult to fully trust the Good Shepherd because of overwhelming dysfunction from other relationships? He is YOUR Good Shepherd and He has good plans for YOU. Read Psalm 23. Replace the words *me, my* and *I* with your name. Renew your mind with the Word of God and align your thoughts with what God says about you.

Heavenly Father, As I meditate on your Word, let it renew my mind. Let me see you in truth instead of the way my wounded heart might portray you. Let me begin to see myself through the lens of your love. In Jesus Name, Amen.

Chapter Four: Receiving God's Free Gift

Rachel attends the student crusade and responds to the love of God. She opens her heart and accepts Jesus as her Savior. Have you accepted Jesus as your personal Savior? John 3:16 reads, *For God so loved the world that He gave His one and only Son, that whoever believes in him will not perish but have everlasting life.* Reflect on your own salvation experience. If you have never accepted Jesus as Savior, you can do so now.

> *Heavenly Father, I accept the free gift of salvation that comes through your son, Jesus Christ.*
>
> *I believe He died on the cross for my sins and was raised from the dead. I accept Jesus as Savior and Lord of my life. In Jesus Name, Amen.*

Chapter Five: Surviving Overwhelming Circumstances

In a few short years, John's life seemed to fall apart. Pressure mounted due to drought, debt, disease. Have you experienced overwhelming circumstances? Have the walls of life seemed to crash in around you? Do you wonder where God is during your struggles?

Jeremiah 29:11 reads, *"For I know the plans I have for you," declares the Lord, "plans to prosper you and not to harm you, plans to give you hope and a future."* Which verses encourage you during difficult times?

> *Heavenly Father, thank you for your Word that gives encouragement when life is overwhelming. I will remember your promises and faithfulness through it all.*
>
> *In Jesus Name, Amen*

Chapter Six: Embracing Contentment In the Waiting

After struggling in the *waiting period* for God's promise to be revealed, Rachel found contentment in trusting. Have you struggled as you have waited for God to act? Have you experienced fear, insecurity, doubt? Rest in His faithfulness as you wait. Reflect on Isaiah 40:31.

> *Heavenly Father, As I wait for your promises to be fulfilled, I will trust. I choose peace and joy during this period. I remember your faithfulness. I trust your heart and your timing.*

In Jesus Name, Amen.

Chapter Seven: Discovering God's Perfect Timing

As Mr. Avery's life is coming to an end, John and Rachel's is just beginning. John realizes that God is working in the midst of tragedy and that He brought Rachel, and Jackson, at the time he needed them most. Ecclesiastes 3:1 tells us that there is a time for everything, and a season for every activity under the heavens. Reflect on a situation in which God's perfect timing was evident in your life.

> *Heavenly Father, Though I don't always understand, I will trust that your timing is perfect and your plans are good. In Jesus Name, Amen.*

Chapter Eight: Relating to a Loving Father

John and Rachel had different frameworks for father. John perceived his Heavenly Father as loving and patient just as his earthly father. As Rachel progressed in her relationship with God, she struggled with the perception that her Heavenly Father was distant and angry just as her earthly father. Though Rachel believed verses that signified God's goodness such as Psalm 34:8, her doubt seemed to stay just below the surface. Read Psalm 34:8 and reflect on your own framework.

> *Heavenly Father, I'm thankful that you are good and that nothing can separate me from your love. Help me to walk daily in that love and trust that you have good plans for me. In Jesus Name, Amen.*

Chapter Nine: Overcoming Quagmire

The mission team encountered quagmire; a soft boggy area of land that gives way underfoot. Have you found yourself sinking in quagmire? Are you "stuck" in one or more area—spiritual, physical, emotional, financial, relational? Jesus wants us to surrender our struggle to Him.

We are told in 2 Corinthians 12:9 that when we are weak, He is strong.

Heavenly Father, I'm struggling with _____. I am stuck. I surrender this area of my life to you. Be my strength when I am weak. I will renew my mind from your Word in regard to this area so that the enemy will have no stronghold.

In Jesus Name, Amen

Chapter Ten: Locking Arms with Friends

John and Rachel received a bad report. They turned to friends for support. Friends who encouraged, friends who prayed, friends who reminded of the faithfulness of God. What does your network of friends look like? Do you have friends who will encourage you in your relationship with God and in His plan for your life? If not, ask Him to cultivate this type of friendship. Read Mark 2:3-4 that reveals acts of true friendship.

Heavenly Father, Send friends who will encourage me to draw closer to you. To trust you despite a bad report. Help me be the friend I want to have.

In Jesus Name, Amen.

Chapter Eleven: Grieving a Loss

Grief is the God-given vehicle to navigate loss. It is not always a straight path to the finish line. Grief can move us forward then spiral back unexpectedly. Have you experienced the loss of a loved one or friend, a relationship, a job, a dream? Are you grieving? Wherever you are in the process, God will give you comfort. Read Psalm 34:18.

Heavenly Father, Help me navigate the loss of _____. Hold my hand through these days and weeks and months ahead.

Hold my heart and my tears. Comfort me in this process. In Jesus Name, Amen.

Chapter Twelve: Trusting in the Waiting

John and Rachel celebrate their first-born's sixteenth birthday. Seventeen years before, after miscarriage, their hope of parenthood was waning. Have you lost hope? Does your promise seem out of reach? Revisit Jeremiah 29:11. Reflect on these words. Plans. Prosper. Hope. Future.

Heavenly Father, When I am hurt, disappointed, disillusioned, help me to keep my eyes on you and trust that you have a plan and are working on my behalf. In Jesus Name, Amen.

Chapter Thirteen: Dealing with Jealousy

In Galatians 5, believers are warned against jealousy and envy. Anastasia confesses that she is jealous of Rachel. It is implied that Rachel is jealous of Anastasia's role in Jackson's life that resulted in his absence from her own. Jealousy and envy can manifest from a desire for love, time, power, position, attention, money or success that someone else possesses. Have you struggled with these?

Heavenly Father, I give you the jealousy and envy I hold today in regard to _____. Help me to always seek you for my needs and never compare myself to others or covet what another possesses. In Jesus Name, Amen.

Chapter Fourteen: Accepting What We Cannot Change

Just four months into marriage with Anastasia, Jackson realized that he entered the relationship with the intent of changing her mind about New Berry. He believed he could convince her to love the place and the people just as he. His lack of success brought disappointment and disillusionment. Have you been disappointed in a similar situation? Did you assume change would come, but it did not? The word *serenity* means the state of being calm, peaceful, and untroubled. Pray the Serenity Prayer over your situation.

> *Heavenly Father, Grant me the serenity to accept the things I cannot change. The courage to change the things I can. And the wisdom to know the difference. In Jesus Name, Amen.*

Chapter Fifteen: Remembering the Faithfulness of God

John and Rachel are confronted with disease progression and brain surgery. In the midst of the unexpected and fear of the unknown, their prayer revisits the faithfulness of God. Remembering past faithfulness of God refocuses our mind to the One who is able and builds our faith to again trust Him. Allow yourself to remember His work in your life. Whether small or great, each act of His faithfulness is worthy of remembrance. Reflect on Isaiah 25:1 and pray this verse back to Him.

> *Heavenly Father, You are my God; I exalt you and praise your name, for in perfect faithfulness you have done wonderful things, things planned long ago.*
> *In Jesus Name, Amen.*

Chapter Sixteen: Surrendering All

Rachel wore her strength, her assurance, like a soldier's armor. Rachel was strong and in control, most days. No one ever saw the tender, vulnerable woman who was sometimes tired, afraid and overwhelmed. Do you keep your deepest struggles hidden? God sees the parts of us that no one else sees as expressed in Psalm 139:1-2. Surrender the innermost parts of yourself to the one who knows you inside and out and will carry you in your darkest days.

> *Heavenly Father, I give you every part of myself. Empower me to face whatever comes my way. In Jesus Name, Amen.*

Chapter Seventeen: Relinquishing the Battle

A small bird knocks over Rachel's framed scripture in her kitchen on the very day the worst news is conveyed from John's doctors. In 2 Chronicles 20:15, God is assuring Rachel that the battle before her belongs to Him. He releases her from that which she was never meant to carry. Are you trying to handle that which belongs to God? Release it now to the One who is our Mighty Warrior.

> *Heavenly Father, I release my battles to you. I know you have already won and have given me the victory. Thank you. In Jesus Name, Amen.*

Chapter Eighteen: Navigating Grief

When John dies, Rachel begins the grief journey. God uses a hawk to remind her that He sees. Are you grieving a loss? Are you facing inconceivable pain or hardship? Meditate on Psalm 34:15. *The eyes of the Lord are on the righteous, and His ears are attentive to their cry.*

> *Heavenly Father, Thank you that no matter what I face, you see me. You are always with me. You hear my cries and hold my tears. Help me to always remember your faithfulness. In Jesus Name, Amen*

Chapter Nineteen: Releasing Anger

Jackson's absence in John's final days turned Rachel's pain to anger, her anger to bitterness. Have you been hurt by someone you loved and trusted? Have anger and bitterness come from that hurt? Ephesians 4:32 instructs to forgive each other just as in Christ God forgave us. If you struggle to forgive, ask God to help you. He will.

> *Heavenly Father, I know it is your will that I forgive and release anger and bitterness from my heart. I want to be obedient. Help*

me to forgive _____ . *Please begin the healing process in my heart and life. In Jesus Name, Amen.*

Chapter Twenty: Avoiding Sin

As Jackson and Rachel embark on a new relationship, physical attraction grows. They realize that even as adults, boundaries must be set in order to avoid sin. *Hebrews 12:1* instructs, *Throw off everything that hinders and the sin that so easily entangles.* Have you struggled with sin in a particular area? What boundaries could you set to avoid the enemy's snare?

> *Heavenly Father, I am struggling with* _____. *Give me wisdom in setting boundaries and strength to maintain these boundaries. Help me to live a life that is pleasing to you. In Jesus Name, Amen.*

Chapter Twenty-One: Trusting Against all Odds

As Rachel's world once again crashes, she visits those who have been praying for her for decades. She is reminded that God still sees her, has plans for her life, and that His promises to her are still alive. Have you lost sight of God's plan for your life? Are you unable to see God working on your behalf? Revisit Romans 8:28. Choose today to trust his faithfulness and to believe that He is a good father who has great plans for you.

> *Heavenly Father, I love you. I am called according to your purpose. I trust that even against all odds, you are working all things for good. In Jesus Name, Amen.*

BLUE MOON
RISING

Bible Verses for Group Discussions
and Individual Reflections

Chapter One: Matthew 11:28-30

Come unto me, all who are weary and burdened, and I will give you rest.
Take my yoke upon you and learn from me.
For I am gentle and humble in heart, and you will find rest for your souls.
For my yoke is easy and my burden light.

Chapter Two: Romans 8:28

And we know that in all things God works for the good of those who love
him, who have been called according to *His* purpose.

Chapter Three: Psalm 23

The Lord is my shepherd, I lack nothing.
He makes me lie down in green pastures,
he leads me beside quiet waters,
he refreshes my soul.
He guides me along the right paths for his name's sake.
Even though I walk through the darkest valley,
I will fear no evil, for you are with me;
your rod and your staff, they comfort me.
You prepare a table before me in the presence of my enemies.
You anoint my head with oil; my cup overflows.
Surely your goodness and love will follow me all the days of my life,
and I will dwell in the house of the Lord forever.

Chapter Four: John 3:16

For God so loved the world, that He gave His one and only Son, that everyone who believes in him shall not perish, but have eternal life.

Chapter Five: Jeremiah 29:11

"For I know the plans I have for you," declares the Lord, "plans to prosper you and not to harm you, plans to give you hope and a future."

Chapter Six: Isaiah 40:31

But they that wait upon the Lord shall renew their strength; they shall mount up with wings as eagles; they shall run, and not be weary; and they shall walk, and not faint.

Chapter Seven: Ecclesiastes 3:1

There is a time for everything, and a season for every activity under the heavens.

Chapter Eight: Psalm 34:8

Taste and see that the Lord is good; blessed is the one who takes refuge in him.

Chapter Nine: 2 Corinthians 12:9

But he said to me, "My grace is sufficient for you, for my power is made perfect in weakness." Therefore I will boast all the more gladly about my weaknesses, so that Christ's power may rest on me.

Chapter Ten: Mark 2:3-4

Some men came, bringing to him a paralyzed man, carried by four of them. Since they could not get him to Jesus because of the crowd, they made an opening in the roof above Jesus by digging through it and then lowered the mat the man was lying on.

Chapter Eleven: Psalm 34:18

The Lord is close to the brokenhearted and saves those who are crushed in spirit.

Chapter Twelve: Jeremiah 29:11

"For I know the plans I have for you," declares the Lord, "plans to prosper you and not to harm you, plans to give you hope and a future."

Chapter Thirteen: Galatians 5:25-26

Since we live by the Spirit, let us keep in step with the Spirit. Let us not become conceited, provoking and envying each other.

Chapter Fourteen: Serenity Prayer

God grant me the serenity to accept the things I cannot change. The courage to change the things I can. And the wisdom to know the difference.

Chapter Fifteen: Isaiah 25:1

Lord, you are my God; I will exalt you and praise your name,
for in perfect faithfulness
you have done wonderful things, things planned long ago.

Chapter Sixteen: Psalm 139:1-4

You have searched me, Lord, and you know me.
You know when I sit and when I rise; you perceive my thoughts from afar.
You discern my going out and my lying down;
you are familiar with all my ways.
Before a word is on my tongue, you, Lord, know it completely.

Chapter Seventeen: 2 Chronicles 20:15

Do not be afraid or discouraged because of this vast army. For the battle is not yours, but God's.

Chapter Eighteen: Psalm 34:15

The eyes of the Lord are on the righteous, and his ears are attentive to their cry.

Chapter Nineteen: Ephesians 4:32

Be kind and compassionate to one another, forgiving each other, just as in Christ God forgave you.

Chapter Twenty: Hebrews 12:1

Therefore, since we are surrounded by such a great cloud of witnesses, let us throw off everything that hinders and the sin that so easily entangles. And let us run with perseverance the race marked out for us.

Chapter Twenty-One: Romans 8:28

And we know that in all things God works for the good of those who love him, who have been called according to *His* purpose.

Resources for Giving

Red Mountain Grace
redmountaingrace.com

Go International
gointernational.org

Generational Missions
Generationalmissions.org

Rena' Averett is an author, educator and encourager—a wife, mother and Mimi. Above all, she is a follower of Jesus Christ. Rena' resides on a farm in Alabama with her husband. They share five children and 14 grandchildren.

In 2020, Rena' retired having served 25 years as a teacher and principal. She asked God to send dreams and ideas in this new chapter of her life. From that prayer, her debut Inspirational Romance novel, Blue Moon Rising, was born.

Though fiction, Blue Moon Rising is inspired by Rena's life journey and is steeped in the promise of Romans 8:28. It is a story of the perfect faithfulness of God...*against all odds.*